A Bride's Story

8

Kaoru Mori

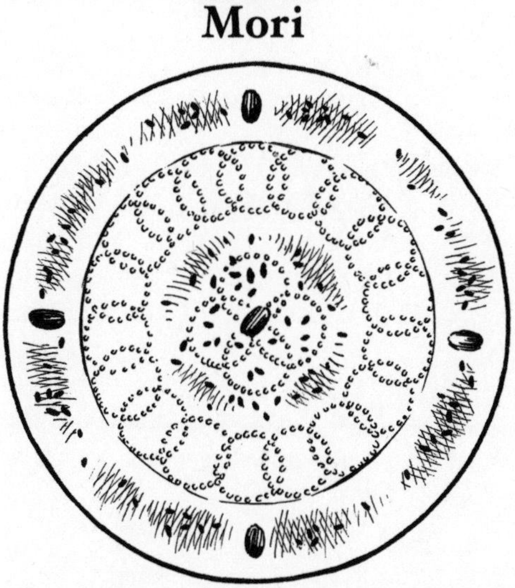

Table of Contents

Chapter 44
ANIS.
SHER-
INE!

GOOD MORNING.
I WAS JUST GATHERING SOME FLOWERS TO BRING YOU.
ROSES?
THEY'RE BEAUTIFUL.
WHAT A LOVELY SCENT.
FLOWERS DON'T LAST...
...BUT THEY'LL KEEP FOREVER...
...IF YOU MAKE ROSE WATER OR SCENTED OILS FROM THEM.
SCENTED OIL?
NOT MUCH TIME HAS PASSED SINCE SHERINE BECAME THE SECOND WIFE OF ANIS'S HUSBAND.

SHERINE SMILES MORE OFTEN...
...AND HER ELDERLY IN-LAWS HAVE SETTLED INTO THEIR NEW LIFE.

Chapter 44
At the Moment a Rose Blooms

AHH...

KO (GULP) こっ
こっ KO
こっ KO
こっ KO

KARA (EMPTY)
......GOODNESS...
SHE NEVER FAILS TO IMPRESS ME WITH HOW MUCH SHE CAN PUT AWAY...
IT'S MESMERIZING JUST WATCHING HER...
SHERINE...
WON'T YOU HAVE SOME MORE?
...ISN'T THIS YOURS?

IT'S ALL RIGHT.
WE STILL HAVE SO MUCH!
HAVE THIS TOO.
EAT AS MUCH AS YOU LIKE!
DIDN'T SHE JUST EAT AN ENTIRE WATER-MELON...
...AND CALL IT AN AFTERNOON SNACK?

YOU'RE VERY GOOD.
......
WOULD YOU LIKE TO PLAY?
OH NO. I'VE NEVER EVEN HELD ONE.
I CAN TEACH YOU.
IT'S SIMPLE ONCE YOU KNOW WHERE TO PUT YOUR FINGERS.

YOU HOLD IT LIKE THIS.
WITH YOUR FINGERS LIKE THIS...

SHER-INE?
SHER-INE?
OH!
THAT'S AMAZING, SHERINE!
HOW DID YOU DO IT?
IT WON'T ALLOW ME TO HOLD IT FOR EVEN A LITTLE WHILE...!
REALLY?
I THOUGHT IT JUMPED ON ANY-ONE'S LAP.
ゴロゴロ GORO (PURR) GORO

MOMI (KNEAD)
モミ
MOMI
モミ
GORO
ゴロ
GORO
ゴロ
GORO
ゴロ
GORO
ゴロ
GORO
ゴロ
GORO
ゴロ
GORO
ゴロ
OH NO!
HE DOES THIS EVERY SINGLE TIME!
....
HE'S NEVER DONE IT TO ME EVEN ONCE.
OH, YOU KNOW CATS...
THE MOMENT THEY HIT SOMETHING PLUMP AND PILLOWY, THEY START...
...MAS-SAG-ING...
...IT...
......
...I DIDN'T MEAN IT IN THAT WAY...
HM?
YES, I KNOW.

SHER-INE?
SHER-INE?
SHER-INE!
YOU GOT IT ROUGH, HUH, SHER-INE?
YOU THINK SO?
WHENEVER YOU'RE ABOUT TO GET SOME ALONE TIME...
...I HEAR THE MISSUS GO ABOUT CALLING, "SHERINE! SHERINE!"
OOPS! COME TO THINK OF IT, YOU'RE "THE MISSUS" TOO NOW, HUH?
SHERINE!
SHERINE!
BAAH!
BAAH!
POWAWAN (GLOWWW)
ポワワン

THAT'S ONE OF THE THINGS THAT MAKES HER SO CUTE.
OHH!
SO THAT'S HOW IT IS, IS IT?
I'VE GONE AND STIRRED THE HORNET'S NEST.
OH! DEAR!
WHAT IS IT?
I JUST WON-DERED WHAT YOU TWO WERE UP TO.
SO I CAME ROUND TO SEE YOU.
NOTHING IN PAR-TICULAR.
RIGHT, SHERINE?

SHERINE, I HOPE YOUR ROOM IS NOT TOO SMALL.
IT IS MORE THAN GENEROUS.
......IT'S SO BIG, MY SON AND I ARE RATHER LOST IN IT, TO BE HONEST.
THEN PERHAPS WE SHOULD BUILD A ROOM WHERE YOU AND ANIS CAN VIEW THE GARDEN TOGETHER.
WHAT DO YOU THINK, ANIS?
A WONDERFUL IDEA!
IF THERE IS ANYTHING YOU NEED...
...DON'T HOLD BACK. TELL ME.
YOU ARE BOTH MY WIVES, AND BOTH OF YOU ARE PRECIOUS TO ME.
IT IS UNSEEMLY TO ALLOW THE MOONLIGHT TO ILLUMINATE A HEAVY SIGH.
TIMES OF JOY ARE THE TIMES WE LIVE.
THUS, THERE IS NAUGHT I WISH FOR MORE THAN A LIFE IN WHICH PEACE REIGNS IN THE HEART.
EXCUSE ME. UNTIL THIS EVENING.

....
HE IS SUCH A FINE MAN.
AND...
...NOT ONLY DOES HE HAVE A GOOD VOICE...
...HE IS ALSO A POET.
HE IS, ISN'T HE?
YES, EXACTLY!
THAT'S SO TRUE!
I'VE ALWAYS THOUGHT EXACTLY THAT!

TELL ME THE TRUTH, MAHFU. HOW ARE THEY?
THE TRUTH ...?
UM...
MAY I ASK WHAT TRUTH YOU'RE ASKING AFTER...?
WELL ...
...ABOUT ANIS AND SHERINE. ARE THEY FRIENDLY?
ARE THEY GETTING ALONG?
OH, DON'T WORRY ABOUT THAT!
YOU KNOW, IF YOU COULD SEE HOW CLOSE THEY ARE, YOU MIGHT EVEN BE JEALOUS...
OOPS...
I SEE.
I'M GLAD TO HEAR IT.
TO TELL THE TRUTH, I'VE BEEN WORRIED.
I KNOW HOW ARDENTLY ANIS DESIRED IT, BUT YOU NEVER KNOW ABOUT THESE THINGS UNTIL YOU'RE IN THE SAME HOUSE.
......

ARE YOU ALL RIGHT WITH THEIR RELATION-SHIP, MASTER?
......
YOUR WIVES HAVE THEIR OWN SPECIAL RELATION-SHIP—THEY ARE AVOWED SISTERS.
......I AM NOT KEEPING SECRETS FROM ANIS, BUT...
...THERE ARE THINGS I TELL ONLY TO MY FRIENDS AS WELL.
AND WOMEN HAVE A WORLD ALL THEIR OWN.
SO I IMAGINE THERE ARE THINGS WOMEN CAN ONLY TELL OTHER WOMEN.
I THINK HAVING A FRIEND SO NEAR AT HAND IS A GOOD THING.

......IT'S NOT THE FIRST TIME I'VE THOUGHT SO...
...BUT ONLY THE MISSUS COULD ATTRACT A HUSBAND LIKE THAT ONE...
MAH-FU?
MAHFU, WHERE ARE YOU?
YES, YES. I'M RIGHT HERE.
AND I'M ALL READY TO GO.

WHAT IS IT, ANIS?
WHAT'S THAT LOOK FOR?
...I'M HAPPY.
WHAT ABOUT?
LOTS OF THINGS.
SOME-TIMES...
...THAT IS, THE THOUGHT HAS OCCURRED TO ME...

ANIS, YOU SIMPLY DON'T TALK ENOUGH.
WHAT WE WANT TO HEAR IS WHAT'S INSIDE YOUR "LOTS OF THINGS."
...HAVEN'T YOU EVER WISHED SHE WOULD SAY MORE?
WELL...
PER-HAPS.
I WOULD LIKE HER TO OPEN UP MORE.
....
....
JUST SAY IT.
WHAT I'M HAPPY ABOUT IS...
...THAT THE TWO OF YOU ARE HERE WITH ME......
YOU, DEAR...
I HOLD YOU IN SUCH HIGH REGARD.
AND WHEN I THINK OF YOU, I'M HAPPY.

AND SO...
...JUST KNOWING THAT YOU ARE THE MAN I LOVE IS THE MOST WONDERFUL FEELING!
I SEE.
AND I FEEL THE SAME FOR YOU, ANIS.

I'M SO HAPPY TO HAVE MET YOU!
AND IT'S LIKE A DREAM THAT WE'RE AVOWED SISTERS!
YOU TOO, SHERINE!
AND SO...
...I THINK......
I FEEL...
....

I LOVE YOU, SHERINE!
GOOD GIRL.
THAT WAS WELL DONE.
Chapter 44: End

SIDE STORY
GAZELLE

PA
(FWIP)
PA
PA
PA

✦ Side Story: End ✦

MY GOD...
THIS IS A TERRIBLE BLOW.
Chapter 45
WHAT A MESS.
WE'LL START TO REBUILD WHERE IT'S DAMAGED LEAST.
LEAVE THE WORST FOR LATER.
...WHAT WILL I DO?
WELL, FIRST LET'S SALVAGE WHAT'S STILL USABLE...
...AND FOR THE TIME BEING, YOU CAN STAY WITH US.

PLEASE COME IN.
YOU CAN USE THIS ROOM.
IT MUST'VE BEEN A SHOCK.
WE HEARD ALL ABOUT IT.
BUT YOU MUSTN'T LET IT DISCOURAGE YOU.
ARE THESE ALL YOUR THINGS?

WE COULDN'T EVEN SALVAGE ANY OF THE CLOTH THAT WE HAD PREPARED FOR PARIYA'S MARRIED LIFE.
OH NO.
YES...
EVERY-THING ELSE BURNED.
ONLY A DAY OR TWO PRIOR...
...THE TOWN CAME UNDER ATTACK BY THE BADAN AND HALGAL CLANS.
PARIYA!
WHERE ARE YOUR MAN-NERS?
PARIYA'S FAMILY CAME TO AMIR'S HOME TO STAY...
...UNTIL THEIR OWN HOME COULD BE REBUILT.
...AMIR, THANK YOU FOR PUTTING US UP.
OF COURSE.
WHAT-EVER WE CAN DO.
THANK YOU FOR YOUR KIND-NESS.

Chapter 45
Pariya's Needlework

THE VERY FIRST FRIEND AMIR MADE WHEN SHE MARRIED INTO A FAMILY IN THIS TOWN...
...WAS PARIYA.

PARIYA WAS OF AN AGE TO BE WED...
...SO THE BIGGEST QUESTION ON HER MIND WAS WHO HER FUTURE HUSBAND WOULD BE.

UN-FORTU-NATELY ...

PARIYA WAS GETTING ANXIOUS ...
HER BRUSQUE PERSONALITY PROVED DISASTROUS.
AND A MATCH WAS NEVER FOUND.
...BUT THEN, VERY RECENTLY, PARIYA MET SOMEONE SHE MIGHT LIKE.

THE TALK WITH THE BOY'S FAMILY DIDN'T GO BADLY...
...BUT WE'LL HAVE TO START REBUILDING HER DOWRY FROM SCRATCH.
AND IT WON'T BE POSSIBLE TO HOLD A WEDDING IN THIS TOWN ANYTIME SOON.
SO IT LOOKS LIKE THE CEREMONY WILL HAVE TO BE DELAYED FOR QUITE A WHILE.
I SEE...
I SUP-POSE IT CAN'T BE HELPED.
IT'S UNFORTUNATE, BUT IT'S THE FACT OF THE SITUATION WE'RE IN. I'M SURE HE'LL WAIT.

I KNEW THIS WOULD HAPPEN.
KNEW WHAT WOULD HAPPEN?
......
YOU KNOW, *THIS*.
NOTHING EVER WORKS OUT FOR ME.
I JUST HAVE TO ACCEPT IT AS FATE.
NOW, THAT ISN'T......
AND I CAN ACCEPT IT!
I ACCEPT THAT I'LL DIE UNMARRIED!
IT ISN'T TRUE.
I KNOW EVERYTHING THAT WAS MADE IS RUINED, WHICH REALLY IS TOO BAD, BUT—
NO! IT'S MY FATE!!

EVEN IF WE FINALLY SET A DAY FOR THE WEDDING...
...THE GROOM WILL GET COLD FEET, OR THE MUSICIANS WILL TAKE A WRONG TURN AND NEVER ARRIVE...
...THEN THE FOOD WILL GET COLD, AND A NEIGHBOR'S MULE WILL COME IN AND KICK OVER ALL THE DECORATIONS! IT'S SURE TO HAPPEN!!
I UNDERSTAND HOW YOU FEEL, BUT YOU HAVE TO STOP OVER-THINKING THIS!
THOSE ARE VERY SPECIFIC DISASTERS...
IT'S ALL RIGHT. HE'LL WAIT FOR YOU.
THIS ISN'T YOUR FAULT, PARIYA.
WE'LL FIND SOMEONE WHO ISN'T BUSY AND ASK HER TO HELP.
......
TILEKE IS VERY GOOD AT SEWING.
URK!

MISS PARIYA...
DON'T YOU LIKE NEEDLE-WORK?
IT'S NOT THAT!
IT ISN'T THAT I DON'T LIKE IT...

MAKE A BIRD! IT'S MORE FUN THAT WAY!
IT ISN'T THAT I DON'T LIKE IT......
IT'S THAT IT JUST WON'T DO WHAT I WANT IT TO DO!
AND I GET SO FRUS-TRATED ......
UM... YEAH.
I GUESS SO.
HM...
SHOW ME.
WHAT KIND OF DESIGN ARE YOU DOING?
GRAND-MOTHER ...

......
WE MAKE CERAMICS, YOU KNOW?
IT MADE MY HUSBAND SO HAPPY, I COULDN'T PREVENT IT.
HE WAS TEACHING HER TO SHAPE CLAY LONG BEFORE SHE EVER HELD A NEEDLE AND THREAD. THAT MAY HAVE BEEN A MISTAKE.
THE ONLY THING SHE DOES WITH REAL PASSION IS MAKE BREAD.
AH! DOUGH IS A LOT LIKE CLAY!
OTHER THAN THAT, SHE HAS NO INTEREST ......
......
HMM, LET'S SEE...
LISTEN, PARIYA...

YOU AREN'T THE DISOBEDIENT CHILD EVERY-ONE SAYS YOU ARE.
I KNOW THAT YOU WERE KIND TO AMIR...
...WHEN SHE FIRST CAME TO US...
...SO I FORESEE YOU FINDING A GOOD MATCH.
BUT...
...EVEN SO, YOU NEED TO LEARN TO HANDLE A NEEDLE.
THIS HAS GIVEN US A GOOD OPPOR-TUNITY.
WELL? ARE YOU WILLING TO BE EDUCATED?

RIGHT!
OKAY, I'M OFF.
WE'LL BE MAKING LUNCH TO BRING TO THOSE FAMILIES AFFECTED.
TORKAN!
SCATTER IT A LITTLE AT A TIME.
ALL OF THEM NEED TO GET SOME!
KARLUK!
DO YOU STILL HAVE AN OPEN STALL?
WE'RE EVEN USING THE GARDENS.
WE'RE COM-PLETELY FULL.
IS THAT SO?
I SUPPOSE I'LL HAVE TO TRY SOMEPLACE ELSE.
I HEAR THERE ARE STILL HORSES DOWN BY THE RIVER TOO.

....
......
YOU'RE THAT TYPE, EH?
YOUR WORK IS INCON-SISTENT.
YOU MISTAKE RAPIDITY FOR SKILL.
HASTY, WITH NO PATIENCE TO SPEAK OF.
THAT'S ...!
THAT'S EXACTLY HOW I AM!
NOTHING I DO GOES RIGHT!
I NEED HELP! WHAT CAN I DO!?
FOR STARTERS, YOU MUST DO EACH AND EVERY STITCH WITH CARE...
...MAKING SURE THEY LINE UP AND ARE ALL OF THE SAME LENGTH.
WITH CARE...?

ONCE YOU BECOME A MOTHER, YOU WILL BE RESPONSIBLE FOR EVERYTHING YOUR FAMILY WEARS...
...SO SEW EACH PIECE AS IF YOUR CHILDREN WERE GOING TO WEAR IT.
WHAT'S MORE, IF YOU HATE WHAT YOU DO, YOU'LL NEVER IMPROVE.
WHAT? YOU CAN'T IMAGINE THAT?
CHILDREN...
ALL RIGHT, THINK OF SOMEONE YOU CARE ABOUT WHEN YOU SEW.
DO THAT, AND YOU'LL IMPROVE.
I THINK OF HAWKS WHEN I DO NEEDLE-WORK.

......
AMIR, WHAT DO YOU THINK OF WHEN YOU'RE STITCHING?
YOU MEAN WHEN I'M ALONE?
YES.
......
A SONG.
WHEN I'M ALONE, I SING.
...IS THAT RIGHT?

THINK OF SOMEONE YOU CARE ABOUT WHEN YOU SEW.
SOME-ONE I CARE ABOUT ...
FATHER
MOTHER
PARI-YA!
HOW WILL I EVER FIND A GROOM WITH YOU LIKE THIS!?
モヤ
MOYA (GLOOM)
PARIYA, CAN'T YOU LET UP A LITTLE?
モヤ
MOYA
AMIR?
GREAT AT EVERY-THING.
URK!
COOKING
HUNTING
STITCHING
WHO?
WHO?

LET ME SEE.
DID YOU FINISH?
THIS IS WELL DONE.
HM.
YOU DID ESPECIALLY FINE WORK IN THIS SECTION, DIDN'T YOU?
OH, IT'S TRUE!
QUITE WONDERFUL!

OH! DID YOU DO THIS, PARIYA?
WELL, GOODNESS. ISN'T THIS BEAUTI- FUL?
ALL THE STITCHES LINE UP. IT'S SO PRETTY!
DEAR!
LOOK AT THIS!
THANK YOU! IT APPEARS YOU SPENT MUCH TIME HELPING MY DAUGHTER SEW.
SHE IS THE ONE WHO STITCHED ALL THIS.
WHAT? IT WAS REALLY HER?
TRULY?
WELL DONE, PARIYA.
YOU REALLY CAN DO IT, PARIYA.
YES! I'VE ALWAYS THOUGHT YOU WERE GOOD WITH YOUR HANDS!
UU!

AFTER WE'VE ALREADY BEEN SUCH A BURDEN ON YOU, FOR YOU TO SPEND SO MUCH EFFORT HELPING PARIYA...
I DON'T KNOW HOW I CAN EVER THANK YOU...
WAIT! MOTHER! THAT'S WAY OVER-BOARD!
WE DIDN'T DO MUCH OF ANYTHING.
THE ONE WHO DID THE WORK WAS THE GIRL HERSELF.
ACTUALLY, ALL I DID WAS TELL HER TO SEW IT WITH SOMEONE IN MIND.
WITH SOMEONE IN MIND?
REALLY...?
THEN WHO DID YOU HAVE IN MIND WHEN YOU MADE THIS?
UM...
IT ISN'T AS IF I HAD ANYONE IN PARTICU-LAR...
HOW TO PUT IT...
IT'S KIND OF LIKE...
NOT ANYONE SPECIFI-CALLY...

HEY! UMAR!
THE HERD IS SCATTERING...
WHY ARE YOU JUST STANDING THERE?
MMM...
HMM? YOU'VE STILL GOT THAT BUSINESS ON YOUR MIND?
WELL, YEAH.
I HEAR IT'S BEEN DELAYED. HOW LONG?
WHAT CAN WE DO? WITH THE SITUATION AS IT IS...

BUT EVEN UNDER NORMAL CONDITIONS, THERE'S STILL A LOT TO TALK OVER.
THESE THINGS ALWAYS TAKE TIME.
STOP TRYING TO RUSH IT.
......BUT EVEN SO...
...IT SEEMS THEY WERE HIT PRETTY HARD.
I HEAR THEY COULD USE A LOT OF HELP.
DO YOU THINK WE COULD HELP THEM?
AS A WAY OF SHOWING OUR SYMPATHIES?
SURE!
LET'S GO!

Chapter 46
To the Northern Plains

YES! THAT'S PERFECT.
LET'S TRY FIRING IT.
DON (BOOM)
BO (WHAM)

THESE ARE WEAPONS CAPTURED FROM THE BADAN.
THEY'RE HIGH QUALITY.
......
IT'S SMALL, BUT IT HAS RANGE.
YES.
IF WE JUST REMAKE THE CARRIAGES FOR THEM, WE CAN USE ALL THESE TOO.
IF THEY CAN BE SALVAGED, THEY MAY COME IN HANDY IF AND WHEN RUSSIA ATTACKS.
I DO STILL WONDER ABOUT THOSE SURVIVING HALGAL...
THEY RELOCATED TO THE NORTHERN PLAINS JUST AS WE TOLD THEM THEY SHOULD.
WE'RE HERE, JORUK.
WAKE UP.

......
I'M STILL SLEEPY.
NO ONE FORCED YOU TO COME.
YOU COULD HAVE STAYED AT THE CAMP...
DON'T EVEN JOKE ABOUT THAT.
I COULDN'T STAY THERE.
YOU KNOW HOW WHINY AND BORING THOSE OLD GEEZERS ARE. TO HEAR THAT DAY AFTER DAY...
....
PERSON-ALLY, I'M SURPRISED WE HAVE THIS MUCH GRAZING GROUND LEFT.
NOBODY ELSE SEEMS TO BE USING IT.

APART FROM US, NOBODY WOULD BE HERE.
WHAT DO YOU EXPECT? EVERYBODY KNOWS THAT RUSSIA WILL ATTACK THIS PLACE ANY-TIME NOW.
I SUP-POSE SO.
IT'S RATHER LIKE WE'VE BEEN ASSIGNED BORDER PATROL.
....
AT LEAST WE'LL BE ABLE TO SURVIVE THIS WINTER.

WITH THE BATTLE LOST AND HIS FATHER DEAD...
...AZEL INHERITED THE CLAN LEADER-SHIP.
THERE WAS NOT A SINGLE DISSENTING VOICE.
HERE.
EAT IT.

YOU'D BETTER FATTEN UP WHILE YOU CAN.
WE NEVER KNOW WHEN FOOD WILL RUN OUT.
WE NEED A NEW WELL.
ALSO SOME NEW GROUNDS WHERE WE CAN SET UP WINTER CAMP.
......
I GET THE FEELING WE'LL GET COMPLAINTS FROM THE LOCALS.
FIND SOME-PLACE, BAIMAT.
BARGAIN WITH THEM DIRECTLY.

JORUK, YOU GO TOO.
YOU'LL BE IN CHARGE OF BRINGING CAMELS AND GOATS TO PASTURE TOO.
ME?
ALL OF THEM? BY MY-SELF?
YOU CAN DO IT.
WE HAVE TO FIND AS MUCH FOOD AS POSSIBLE WHILE THE SUN LASTS.
....
GUESS IT'S NOT LIKE I'VE GOT SOMETHING BETTER TO DO.
WE'VE SPARED THEIR LIVES AND LEFT THEM THEIR LIVE-STOCK.
BUT THAT DOESN'T MEAN WE'VE FORGIVEN THEM.

AT SOME POINT RUSSIA WILL ATTACK— ALL WE CAN DO IS HOPE THAT THE HALGAL WILL BUY US TIME.
WHAT HAPPENS IF THE HALGAL GET IN BED WITH THE RUSSIANS?
WE HAVEN'T SIMPLY SET THEM LOOSE.
WE'LL SEND PEOPLE TO CHECK ON THEM EVERY NOW AND THEN.
......
BE-SIDES...
...I FIND IT HARD TO BE-LIEVE...
...THOSE MEN WOULD ALLY THEMSELVES WITH RUSSIA.
WE'LL KEEP OUR EYES ON THINGS FOR A WHILE.

✦ Chapter 46: End ✦

COTTON, HEMP...
...SILK...
...AND SILK THREAD...
✦ Chapter 47 ✦
THAT SHOULD BE ENOUGH FOR EVERYTHING YOU NEED.

OH... IT'S FAR TOO MUCH!
WE'LL REPAY YOU WHEN WE'RE SETTLED.
I CAN'T THANK YOU ENOUGH!
IT'S JUST WHAT WE'VE BEEN ABLE TO GATHER FOR TILEKE'S DOWRY.
AND THERE'S PLENTY OF TIME YET BEFORE TILEKE WILL ACTUALLY NEED IT.
PLEASE FEEL FREE TO USE IT...
...MISS PARIYA.
TH...
THANK YOU.
....
DOESN'T SHE ALSO NEED LEATHER?

LEATHER?
YOU CAN DO NEEDLE-WORK ON HIDE?
YES. YOU CAN MAKE...
...MIRROR HOLDERS OR SADDLES.
WE DON'T EMBROIDER LEATHER IN THESE PARTS.
YOU DON'T?
EH!?
I'VE NEVER HEARD OF IT EITHER!
ER... SO YOU REALLY ...?
AH... NO-BODY DOES IT?
AT ANY RATE...
SO, YOU CAN DO NEEDLE-WORK ON LEATHER?
YOU CERTAINLY CAN!
BUT A NORMAL NEEDLE WON'T PASS THROUGH, WILL IT?

Chapter 47
The Comb Holder

WHEN A BRIDE TAKES A HUSBAND...
...SHE BRINGS WITH HER A LARGE QUANTITY OF EMBROIDERED TEXTILES FOR DAILY USE.
SHE STARTS DOING EMBROIDERY WORK LONG BEFORE SHE COMES OF MARRIAGEABLE AGE.
IT'S A LONG TRADITION, AND WITHOUT A COMPLETE SET OF EMBROIDERED CLOTH, A GIRL IS NOT CONSIDERED ELIGIBLE TO BE MARRIED.
NATURALLY PARIYA ALSO DID THIS.
BUT IT NEVER GOT VERY FAR.
BUT BECAUSE OF THE DAMAGE TO THEIR HOUSE IN THE RECENT ATTACK...
...THE EMBROIDERY WORK SHE HAD FINISHED WAS DESTROYED.
THE ONLY ONE THAT SURVIVED WAS THIS.
WE'LL HAVE TO START EVERYTHING ELSE FROM SCRATCH.
......
HOW MUCH DO YOU PLAN ON RE-MAKING?
I'D LIKE TO REMAKE AS MUCH AS WE CAN...
...BUT I DON'T WANT TO DELAY THE WEDDING FOR TOO LONG.

ABOUT FORTY DIFFERENT TYPES, SO A TOTAL OF ABOUT A HUNDRED ...?
......
......I SUPPOSE THAT'S ABOUT THE LEAST A GIRL WOULD WANT.
MAKES SENSE.
......
BUT IT SOUNDS LIKE IT WILL TAKE QUITE A LOT OF TIME.
RUSHING THROUGH THEM, PERHAPS THREE OR FOUR YEARS.
I COULD SEE IT TAKING EVEN LONGER.
EVEN SO, LOOKING AT WHAT PARIYA EMBROIDERED BEFORE...
NOW THAT SHE CAN DO BETTER...
...I THINK IT'S GOOD THAT SHE HAS A CHANCE TO DO IT OVER......
OH, COME ON! MOTHER!?
AFTER I PUT SO MUCH WORK INTO THAT!?
BUT AT YOUR WEDDING, EVERYONE WILL SEE IT!
DON'T YOU WANT EVERYONE TO THINK YOU'RE A GOOD BRIDE?
I'D RATHER YOU NOT HAVE ANY PAINFUL MEMORIES OF THAT DAY.

IT'S TRUE...
PEOPLE WILL TALK ABOUT THAT FOR A LONG TIME.
BUT...
...WHO WOULD WAIT THAT LONG FOR ME?
IF I GET ANY OLDER...
...THE "NEXT ONE" MIGHT NEVER COME......
......
YOU'LL BE FINE.
YOU'LL BE FINE, SO...
...JUST DO YOUR BEST.
IT'S TRUE! IT IS LEATHER!
WHAT IS IT?
IT'S A HOLDER FOR SHEEP SHEARS.
IT'S GOT A SAVAGE LOOK!
IT'S VERY STRONG.
GICHICHI (TUGGG)
ギチチ

A COMB HOLDER?
AMIR...
I THOUGHT I'D START ON SOMETHING EASY, AT LEAST.

WHAT DESIGN ARE YOU USING?
I WAS THINKING ABOUT THAT RIGHT NOW...
A COMB HOLDER, HM?
HM... HM...
THERE'S THIS...
HOW ABOUT TRYING TO STITCH SOMETHING LIKE THIS?
URK!
I DON'T THINK I CAN!
IT'S SO COMPLI-CATED!
IF YOU RUN AWAY FROM SOMETHING JUST A LITTLE COMPLEX, YOU'LL NEVER IMPROVE.
I'M CONFIDENT YOU CAN MAKE SOMETHING LIKE THIS WELL.

I THOUGHT I COULD JUST DO SOMETHING SIMPLE...
...BUT IT DOESN'T LOOK LIKE I'LL GET AWAY WITH IT......
STILL, SHE DIDN'T SAY I SHOULD DO EXACTLY THAT DESIGN...
...SO HOW ABOUT SOMETHING SORT OF SIMILAR...
IF ALL YOU THINK OF IS FINDING THE EASY WAY OUT...
...YOU WILL NEVER GET ANY GOOD AT THIS.
AH!

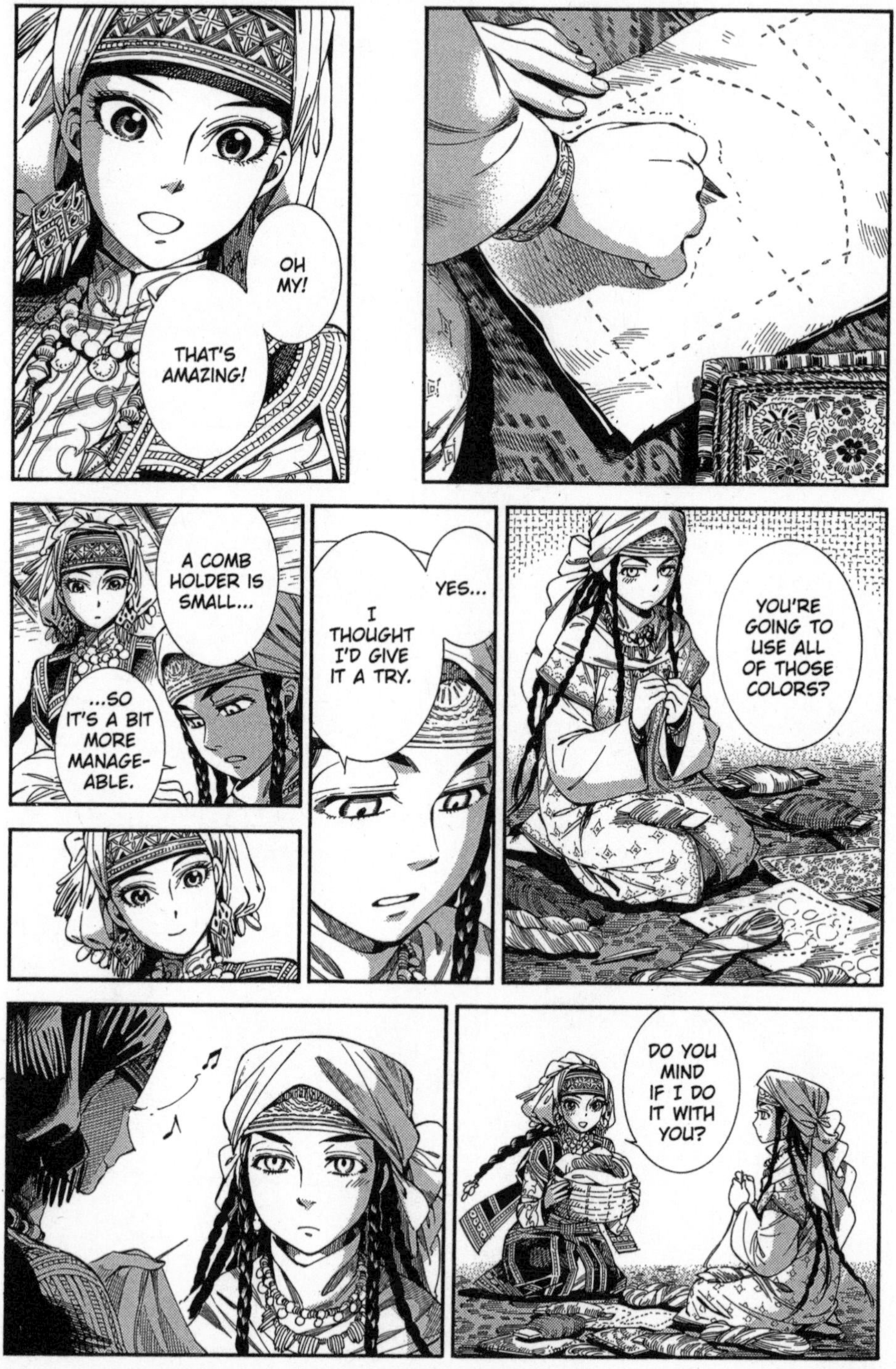
OH MY!
THAT'S AMAZING!
A COMB HOLDER IS SMALL...
...SO IT'S A BIT MORE MANAGE-ABLE.
YES...
I THOUGHT I'D GIVE IT A TRY.
YOU'RE GOING TO USE ALL OF THOSE COLORS?
DO YOU MIND IF I DO IT WITH YOU?

UGH......
I'M ALREADY SICK OF THIS......
MAYBE I CAN SWITCH TO AN EASIER PATTERN NOW...
BUT IF I DO...
HM.
LET ME SEE. YES. YOU'RE MAKING GOOD PROGRESS.
GOOD, GOOD.

I GUESS...
...IT'S BETTER...
...TO MAKE THE BEST STUFF YOU CAN.
....
WOW! INCREDIBLE!
I NEVER KNEW YOU WERE THIS GOOD AT EMBROIDERY!
PARI-YA...
I HAD NO IDEA YOU WERE SO AMAZING!
I'LL BE A LUCKY MAN TO MARRY YOU!
YOU WILL BE MY WIFE, RIGHT?
I DON'T CARE HOW OLD YOU GET!
EH HEH HEH.
SEE WHAT A FINE BRIDE HAS ENTERED MY FAMILY?
I'LL BET YOU'RE ALL JEALOUS NOW!

AHEM...
YOU REALIZE THIS IS A WOMAN'S ROOM, RIGHT?
BOYS MUST NEVER SNEAK INTO PLACES LIKE THIS!
IT'S FINE.
IT'S FINE.
AH! ROSTEM!
I WAS WONDER-ING WHERE YOU'D SNUCK OFF TO!!

DA (DASH)
ダッ
HEY! STOP RIGHT THERE!
YOU STILL HAVE CHORES TO DO IN THE GARDEN!
ROS-TEM!
......

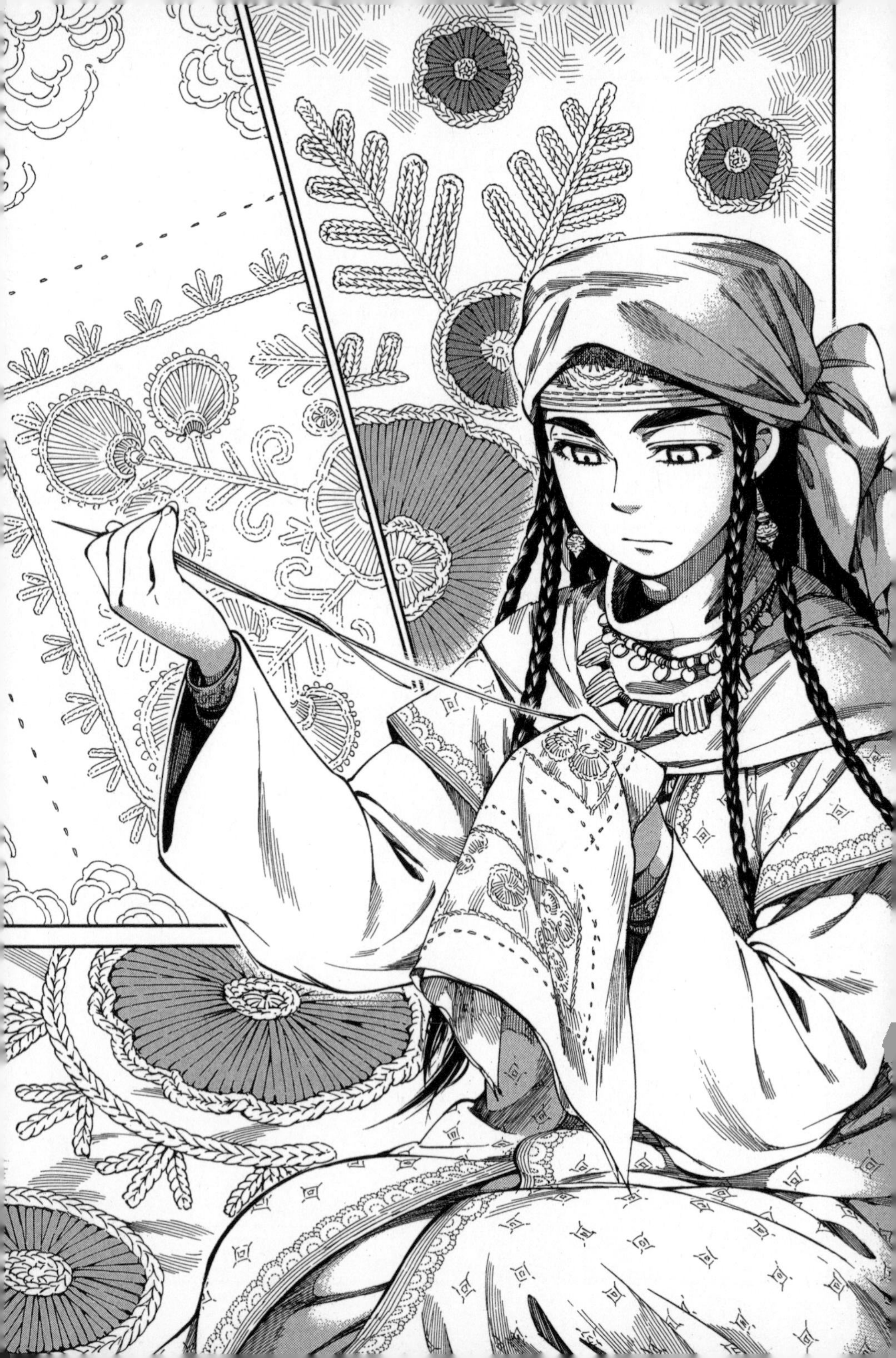

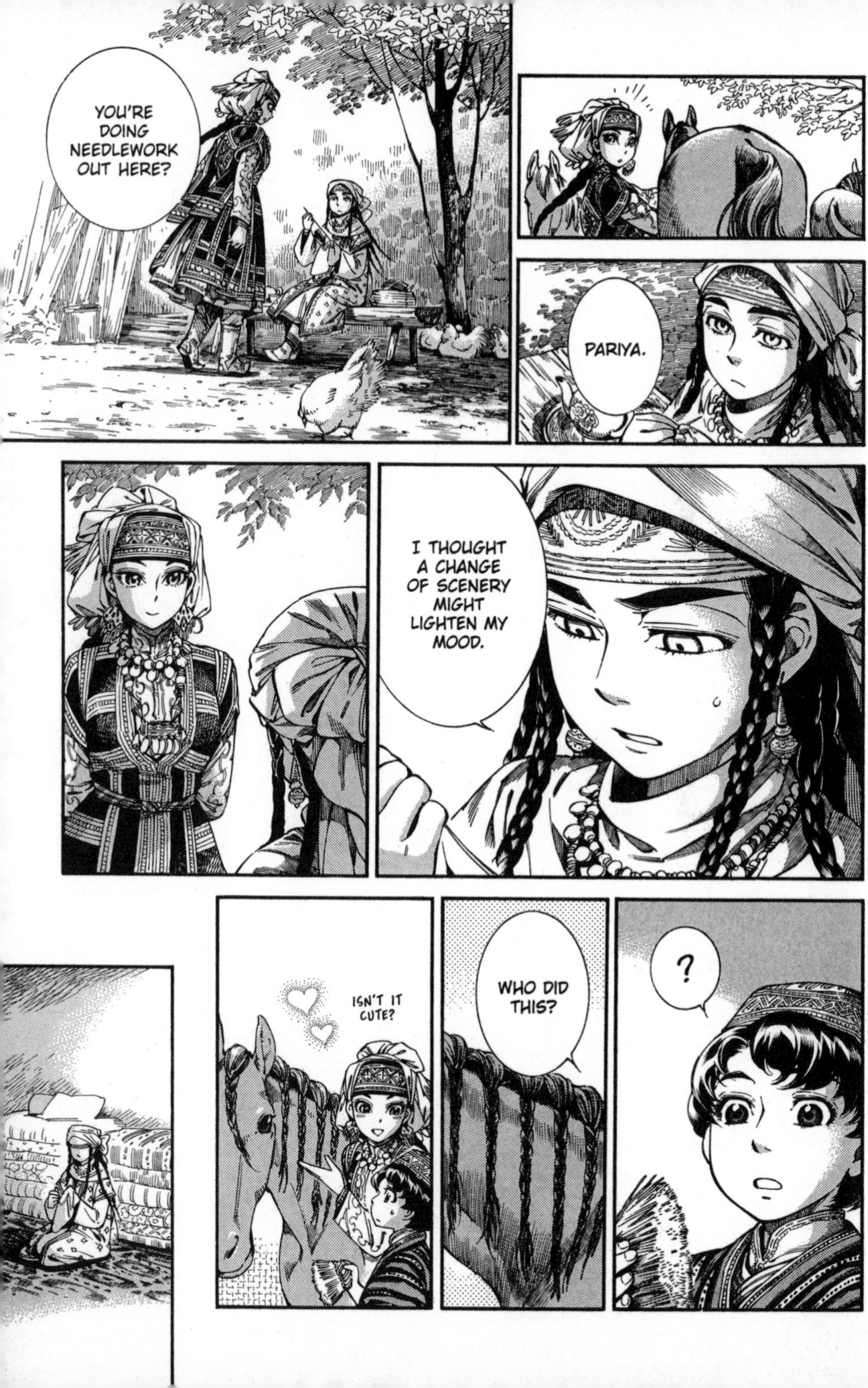

YOU'RE DOING NEEDLEWORK OUT HERE?
PARIYA.
I THOUGHT A CHANGE OF SCENERY MIGHT LIGHTEN MY MOOD.
?
WHO DID THIS?
ISN'T IT CUTE?

WOW! JUST WHAT I'D EXPECT FROM YOU!
AHH...
......
PACHI (SNIP)
パチ

IT'S DONE...
....
I DID MY BEST...
I'VE NEVER TRIED THIS HARD...
THERE'S STILL SO MUCH...
...LEFT TO DO.
NH...

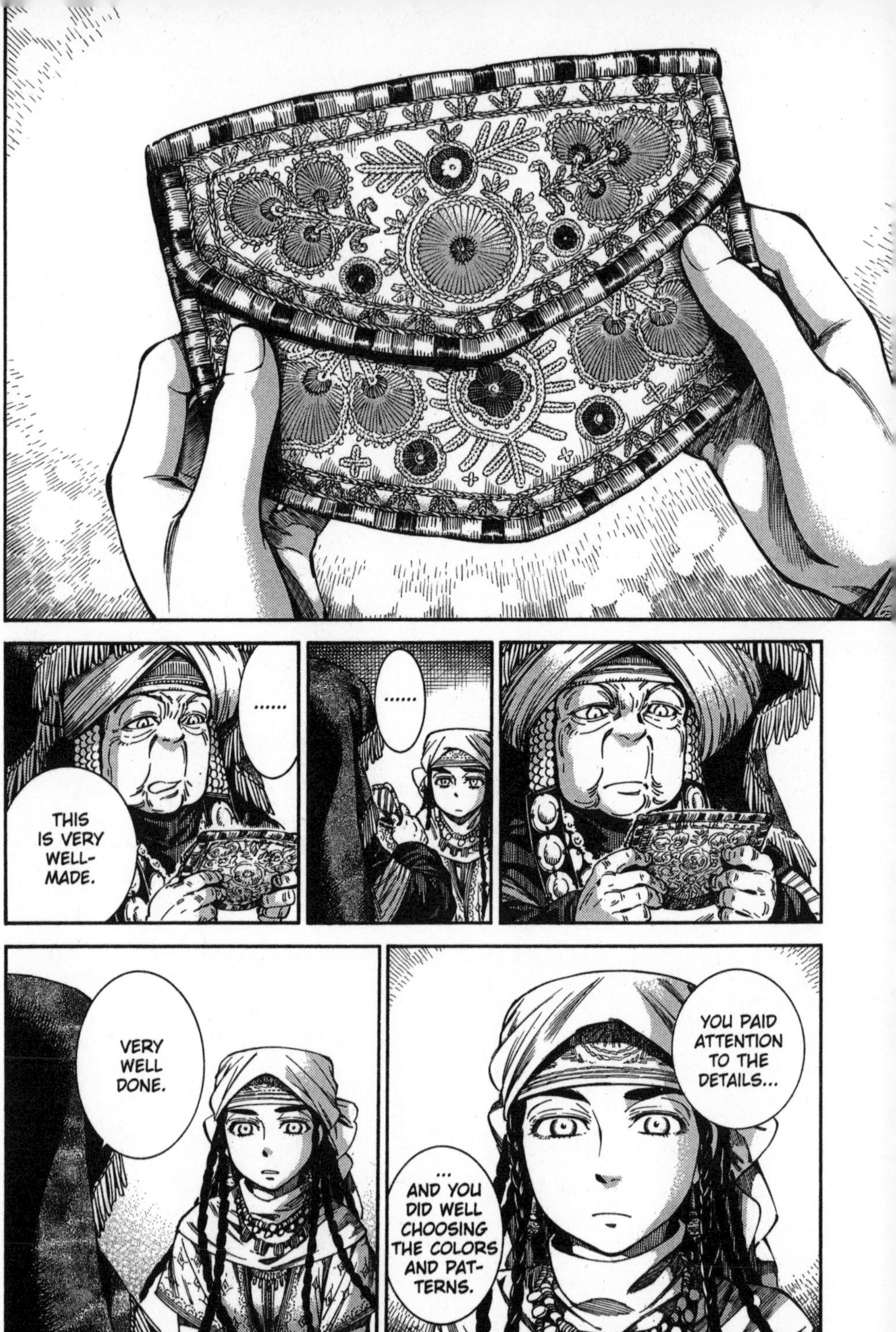
......
......
THIS IS VERY WELL-MADE.
YOU PAID ATTENTION TO THE DETAILS...
...AND YOU DID WELL CHOOSING THE COLORS AND PATTERNS.
VERY WELL DONE.

IT'S VERY PRETTY!
BUT...
...THERE'S STILL SO MUCH MORE LEFT TO DO...
STARTING IS THE HARDEST PART.
THE MORE EMBROIDERING YOU DO, THE EASIER IT WILL BECOME.
BESIDES...
...YOU'LL BE USING THIS EVERY DAY.
EVERY TIME YOU SEE IT, YOU'LL SEE HOW WELL YOU MADE IT.

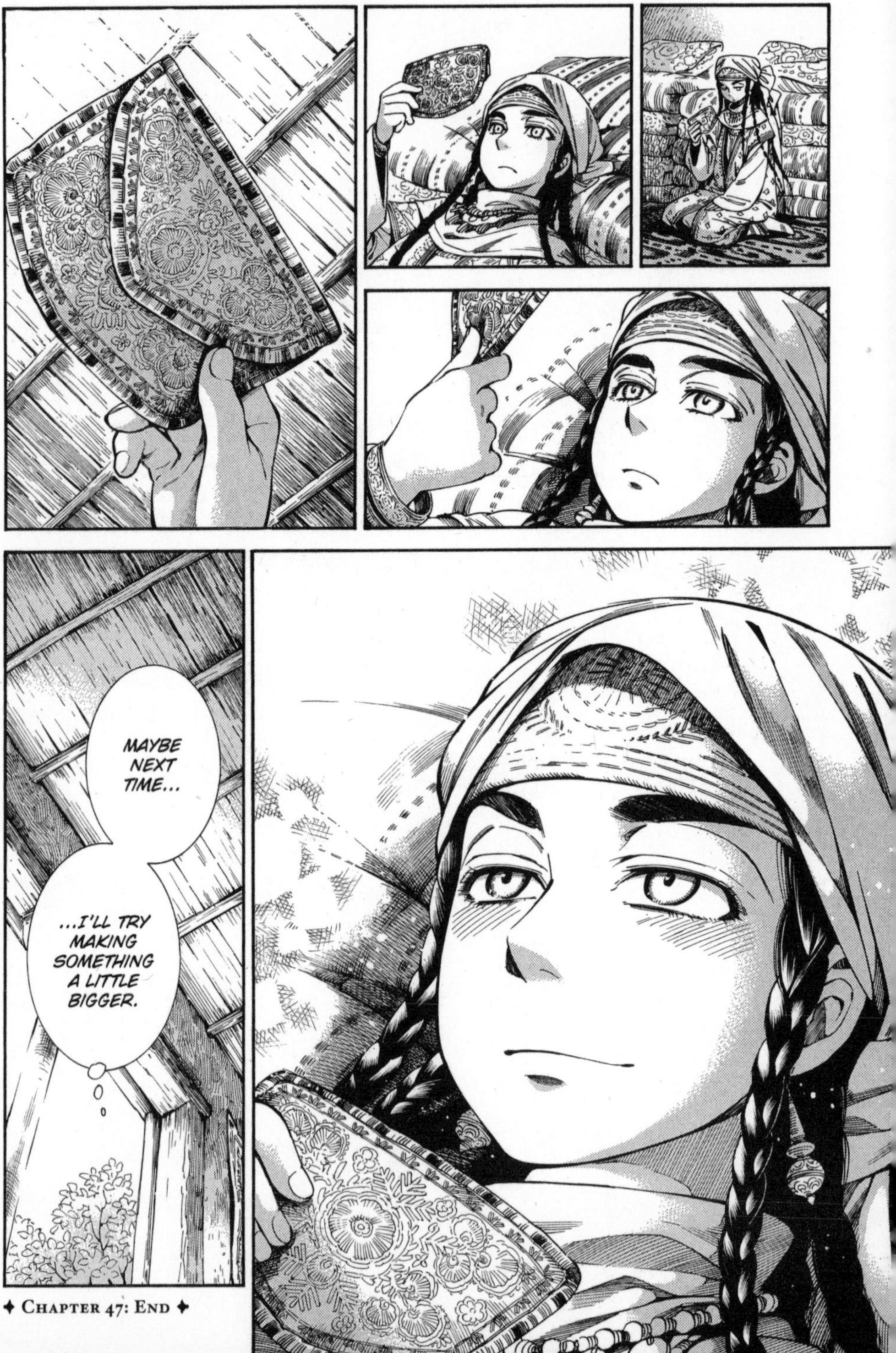
MAYBE NEXT TIME...
...I'LL TRY MAKING SOMETHING A LITTLE BIGGER.

✦ Chapter 47: End ✦

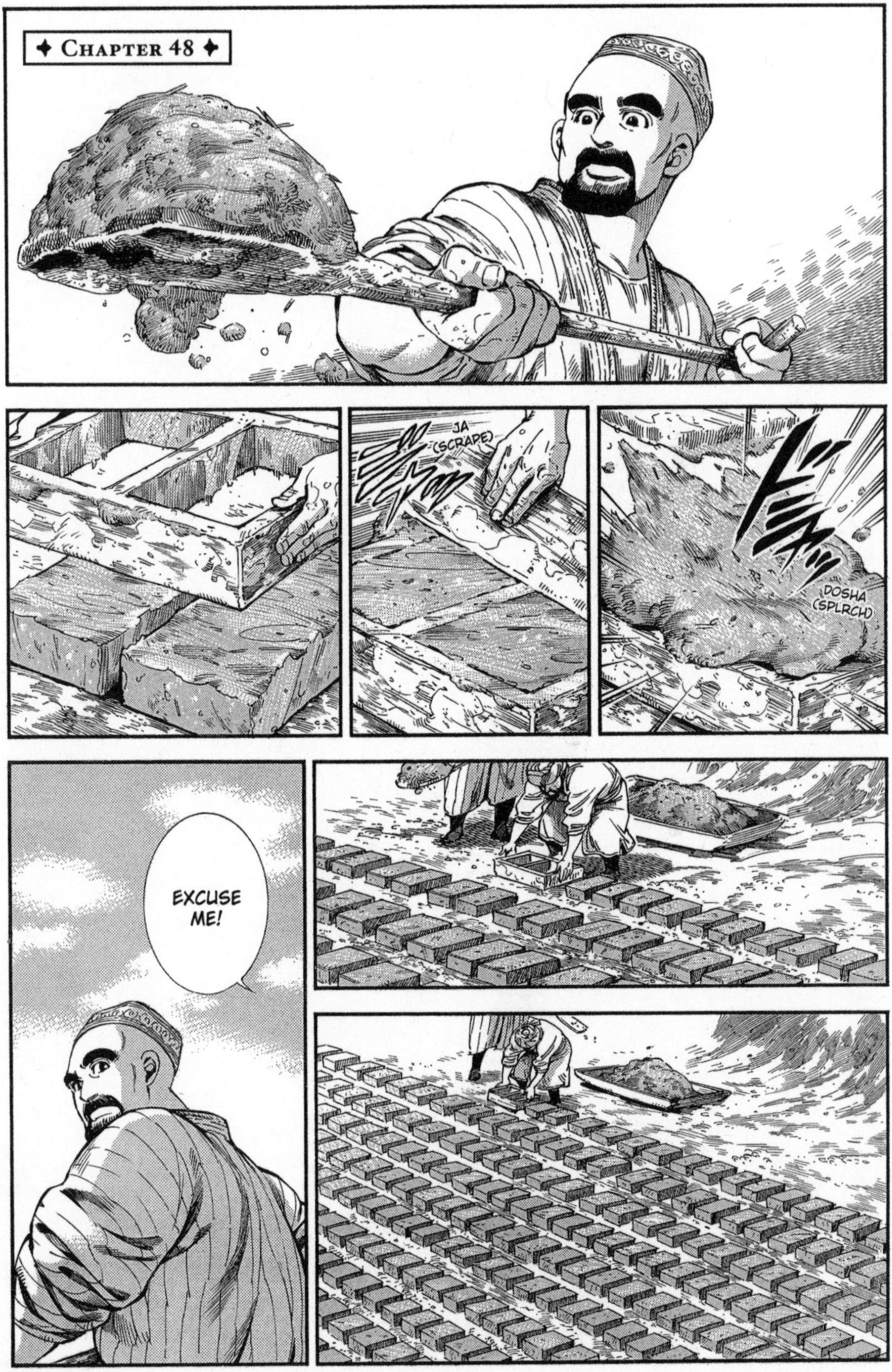

✦ Chapter 48 ✦
JA (SCRAPE)
DOSHA (SPLRCH)
EXCUSE ME!

WE'RE HERE FOR ANY BRICKS YOU MIGHT HAVE FINISHED.
AH.
THE ONES STACKED UP OVER THERE ARE READY TO GO.
HOW ARE THINGS SHAPING UP?
WE'VE MANAGED TO SEAL MOST OF THE HOLES IN THE ROOFS.
BUT WE'VE STILL GOT FOUR OR FIVE HOUSES IN NEED OF MAJOR REPAIRS.
I SEE...
I HOPE IT'S AT LEAST PARTIALLY FINISHED BEFORE WINTER COMES.

KARLUK?
OH, YUSUF!
WHERE ARE YOU HEADED?
THIS GUY'S BEEN COOPED UP ALL THIS TIME...
...SO I THOUGHT I'D LET HIM STRETCH HIS LEGS A BIT.
YOU'VE BEEN TAKING CARE OF ALL THOSE HORSES BY YOUR-SELF...
HAVE YOU BEEN MANAGING ON YOUR OWN?
OH, I'M FINE.
TORKAN AND THE OTHER CHILDREN HELP.

WHO'S THAT?
SOME-BODY'S RELA-TIVE?
....
OH!!
WELL, WELL! YOU'RE VERY WELCOME, COMING SO FAR!

I SEE IT'S WORSE THAN WE IMAGINED.
I'M SORRY FOR WHAT YOU'VE BEEN THROUGH.
YES...I'M AFRAID IT'S BEEN A DISASTER.
YOU DESERVE A KING'S WELCOME, BUT I...
I DON'T EVEN HAVE A HOUSE TO INVITE YOU INTO.........
NO! DON'T MIND US!
WE ONLY DROPPED BY TODAY TO SEE IF WE COULD FIND SOMETHING TO DO TO HELP OUT.
I EXPECT YOU NEED ALL THE HANDS YOU CAN GET, RIGHT?
EH? YOU'RE HERE TO HELP?
SURE! WE'LL DO ANYTHING, JUST SAY THE WORD.
OH MY.
THANK YOU SO VERY MUCH...

EH?
YOU'RE GOING TO USE THIS AS FIRE-WOOD?
WELL, THEY WERE GOING TO BURN IT ANYWAY...
...SO I BROUGHT IT HERE.
IT'S NO GOOD!
IT'S FAR TOO BIG FOR THE—
BEKI (CRACK)
JUST BREAK IT DOWN. IT'LL FIT.
BEKI
BACHI (SNAP)

PARIYA! PARIYA!
PEOPLE FROM THE HOUSE OF YOUR INTENDED HAVE COME TO HELP!
THE HOUSE OF MY WHAT?
YOU KNOW! THE ONES WHO CAME HERE BEFORE ...?
AND YOUR MARRIAGE TALKS WENT SO WELL?
THE BOY!
WHAT'S HIS NAME? OH, UMAR!
HE'S COME TOO!

Chapter 48
Umar Is Here

THAT BOY IS IN TALKS TO MARRY PARIYA!
WHAT? YOU MEAN *THAT* PARIYA!?
I WONDER WHAT KIND OF WORK HIS FAMILY DOES.
ANY SIBLINGS? OR PROMINENT RELATIVES? IS HE AN ONLY CHILD?
WHERE DOES HE LIVE?
HE LOOKS A BIT TOO THIN, DON'T YOU THINK?
HE LOOKS A RESPONSIBLE SORT TO ME. NOT A BAD CHOICE.
HER MOTHER MUST BE SO RELIEVED THAT THEY FINALLY FOUND A MATCH.
WE'LL CERTAINLY NEED AN INTRODUCTION SOMETIME SOON.
WHAT ARE YOU DOING, GOSSIPING OVER HERE?
LET'S SEE...
WHAT SHOULD WE HAVE YOU DO?
...WHAT CAN YOU DO?
I CAN DO A LOT OF THINGS.
WATCH SHEEP. CARRY WATER. MAKE BRICKS.

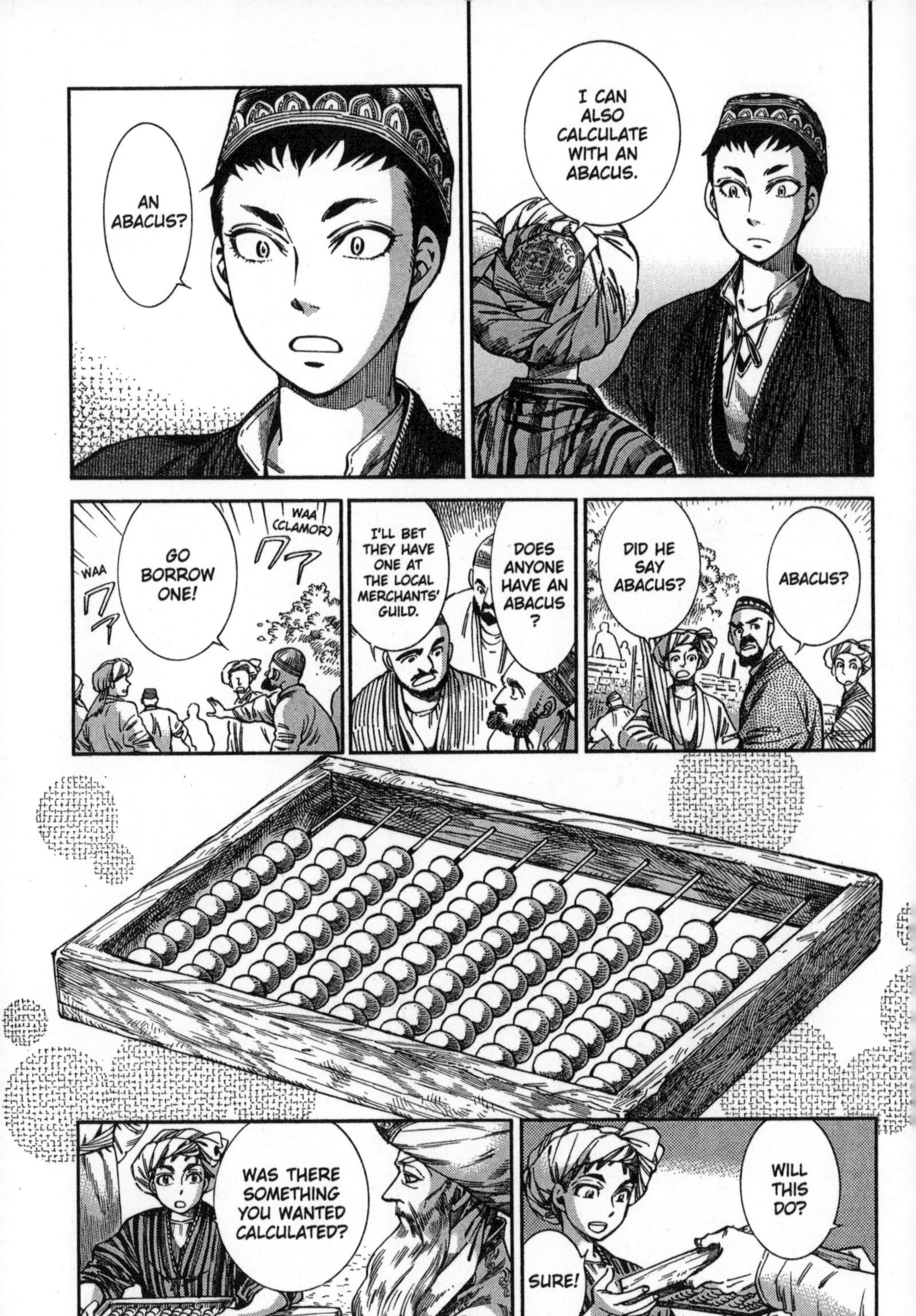
I CAN ALSO CALCULATE WITH AN ABACUS.
AN ABACUS?
ABACUS?
DID HE SAY ABACUS?
DOES ANYONE HAVE AN ABACUS?
I'LL BET THEY HAVE ONE AT THE LOCAL MERCHANTS' GUILD.
WAA (CLAMOR)
ワァ
GO BORROW ONE!
WAA
ワァ
WILL THIS DO?
SURE!
WAS THERE SOMETHING YOU WANTED CALCULATED?

WELL, LET'S SEE...
WHERE ARE THE TOWN MEETING MIN-UTES?
WHAT WITH OUR RECENT TROUBLES, MUCH OF THE COMMUNITY'S PROPERTY HAS BEEN LOST AS WELL.
WE'VE MADE A LIST OF THE REPLACE-MENTS THAT NEED TO BE BOUGHT.
CAN YOU ADD UP THE ESTI-MATES?
YES, SIR.
FIRST, THERE ARE THE GREAT POTS FOR FEASTS...
THEY'RE FOUR TANGA EACH, AND WE NEED THREE.
WE NEED PLATTERS AND TABLE-WARE FOR PARTIES.
THAT'S ABOUT TWENTY TANGA.
KAKA (TAKKA)
KAKO (TOKK)
KAKOKO KAKO
BANNERS FOR FUNERALS, FIFTEEN TANGA.
AND THESE CEREMONIAL ITEMS...
KAKO

AND A WATER CART FOR THE COMMUNAL WATER SUPPLY, THIRTY TANGA.
FIVE TRANS-PORT CARTS...
...ADDING EVERYTHING SO FAR, HOW MUCH DOES IT COME TO?
......
......YOU CAN WRITE TOO?
IT COMES TO THIS MUCH.
YES.
I SEE.
ABOUT WHAT I FIGURED.
YOU'RE QUICK!
WHERE'D YOU LEARN THAT?
WE USED TO RUN A TRADING POST.
I LEARNED IT FROM SOME OF OUR REGULAR TRADERS.
REAL-LY...?
COULD YOU FIGURE OUT MY YEARLY INCOME?
I SOLD SOME SHEEP RECENTLY. CAN YOU CHECK TO SEE IF I GOT A GOOD PRICE?
THE PRICE OF WHEAT HAS GONE UP, SO WHICH SHOP WILL BE THE BEST DEAL?

HOLD ON.
HE'S COME TO HELP THE TOWN, SO TOWN BUSINESS COMES BEFORE PERSONAL MATTERS.
THIS IS PERFECT. WE NEED TO TAKE AN INVENTORY OF WHAT LUMBER AND METAL WE HAVE ON HAND.
HAVING SOMEONE WHO CAN DO QUICK CALCULATIONS WILL BE A GREAT HELP.
WHO HERE CAN WRITE?
I CAN.
TAKE UMAR WITH YOU AND START LOOKING INTO IT.
WE'LL POOL RESOURCES IF WE NEED TO.
UMAR?
I'M COUNTING ON YOU.
YES, SIR!

THEY SAY HE'S ABLE TO USE AN ABACUS.

SO HE CAN DO THAT TOO?
HE'S VERY FAST.
I WAS IMPRESSED.
HE SAYS HE HAS RELATIVES IN THE NEXT TOWN OVER, SO FOR A WHILE HE'LL BE ABLE TO HELP OUT HERE DURING THE DAY.
WELL, WE SHOULD AT LEAST BRING HIM A GIFT OR TWO.
PARIYA, BRING HIM SOME BREAD AND FRUIT.
EH!?
NO!
THEN THIS IS YOUR PERFECT CHANCE!
AN APOLOGY WILL TAKE CARE OF THE WHOLE MATTER!
WAA
I'LL LOAN YOU SOME NICE CLOTHES!
EXACTLY! PUT ON SOME PROPER CLOTHES AND GO!
HE'S COME ALL THIS WAY, RIGHT? GO AND SEE HIM!
WAA (CHATTER)
I...
I MEAN...
I SAID SOME TERRIBLE THINGS TO HIM BEFORE...
HOW CAN I FACE HIM NOW...?

......
WOW.
YOU'RE PRAC-TICALLY GLOW-ING.
......
HERE...
GUI (SHOVE)
GUI
... THANK YOU.
A- ALSO... UM...
UH...
LAST TIME...
I...
I-I- I-I- I-I...
YOUR EYE?

WHEN WE MET BEFORE...
I'M SORRY.
....
ABOUT WHAT?
EH!?
NO, I MEAN... YOU KNOW... BACK WHEN WE MET...
I...
I SAID SOME AWFUL THINGS...
...AND PUSHED YOU...
...AH!
O-OH!
I JUST THOUGHT I'D CAUGHT YOU IN A BAD MOOD.
WELL...
IT WAS THE MOOD, BUT...
...THAT'S STILL...

BUT IF YOU'RE...
うにゃ
MUNYA (MUMBLE)
むにゃ
MUNYA
...NOT OFFENDED OR ANY-THING...
...I'M HAPPY TO HEAR IT, BUT......
I HEAR ALL THE STUFF YOU PREPARED WAS BURNED UP, HUH?
WELL ...
YEAH.
I'M GOING TO HAVE TO MAKE IT ALL OVER AGAIN......
...IS THAT RIGHT?
......

BUT...
BUT MAKING IT ALL OVER AGAIN MEANS...
...THAT ...
...THIS TIME...
...I CAN MAKE IT BETTER THAN I DID BEFORE.
AFTER ALL, EVERYONE WILL SEE THEM...
...SO I WANT TO MAKE SURE I DO THEM PROPERLY.
THEY'RE PRETTY IMPOR-TANT...
...SO I DON'T THINK I SHOULD JUST RUSH MY WAY THROUGH THEM...
I THINK THE WHOLE EXPERIENCE MIGHT NOT BE ALL BAD...
I-I MIGHT HAVE NEEDED THIS TO GET BETTER AT MY EMBROIDERY...
SO MAYBE ...
MAYBE IT'S ACTUALLY BETTER THAT THINGS TURNED OUT THIS WAY...
ER... HUH?
NO. NO, IT ISN'T. I TAKE THAT BACK...

....
HOW LONG DO YOU THINK IT'LL TAKE YOU TO REMAKE IT ALL?
......
....
....
PROBA-BLY...
THREE... MAYBE FOUR YEARS...
THAT LONG!?
NO!
IT WOULD TAKE THAT LONG IF I WERE TO TAKE MY TIME ON IT, BUT...
...I'LL DO IT AS FAST AS I CAN, SO IT WON'T TAKE THAT LONG!

I WILL DO...
...EVERY-THING I CAN TO GET IT FINISHED IN RECORD TIME......
......
IS THAT RIGHT?
....

I'LL BE BACK AGAIN TOMOR-ROW.
SEE YOU!
EH?
UM...
OKAY.
DID YOU GIVE IT TO HIM?
WHAT DID HE SAY?

NOTHING.
JUST THAT HE'D COME AGAIN TOMORROW.
I SEE.
I HOPE SO.
NEGOTIATIONS WERE GOING SO WELL...
AND YOU HAVE TO BE VERY CAREFUL NOT TO BE RUDE!
I'LL BE BACK AGAIN TOMORROW.

✦ CHAPTER 49 ✦

THAT'S AMAZING! AMAZING!!

SUTO
(THWMP)

Chapter 49
A Long Day Trip for Two

DO
DO (CLOP)
DO
HFF!
HFF!
HFF!
NO NEED TO PUSH YOURSELF, SULKEEK.
HFF!
HFF!
HFF!
IT'S BEEN A WHILE FOR SULKEEK.
I DID MANAGE TO RUN ARAKRA RECENTLY THOUGH.
DON (BAM) DON
I MUCKED OUT HIS STALL EVERY DAY...
...BUT I COULD TELL HE WAS IRRITABLE, KICKING THE WALLS AND SUCH.
I'M SORRY I COULDN'T SEE TO YOU...
...SUL-KEEK.

JUST SO YOU KNOW...
...I HAVEN'T FORGOTTEN YOU EITHER, KARLUK.
EH?
DON'T WORRY ...
... ABOUT ME.
I'M FINE.
WHAT ELSE COULD YOU DO AFTER PARIYA AND HER FAMILY LOST THEIR HOME?
EVERY-ONE'S BUSY THESE DAYS.
THERE'S SO MUCH THAT HAS TO BE DONE......
......
!

AMIR!
HOW ABOUT YOU AND I RACE TO THAT TREE?
WHAT DOES THE WINNER GET?
HUH!?
LET'S SEE...
THE WINNER GETS TO ASK THE LOSER FOR ONE THING—ANYTHING!!
HYAH!
DO (GALLOP)
DO
DO
DO
DO
DO

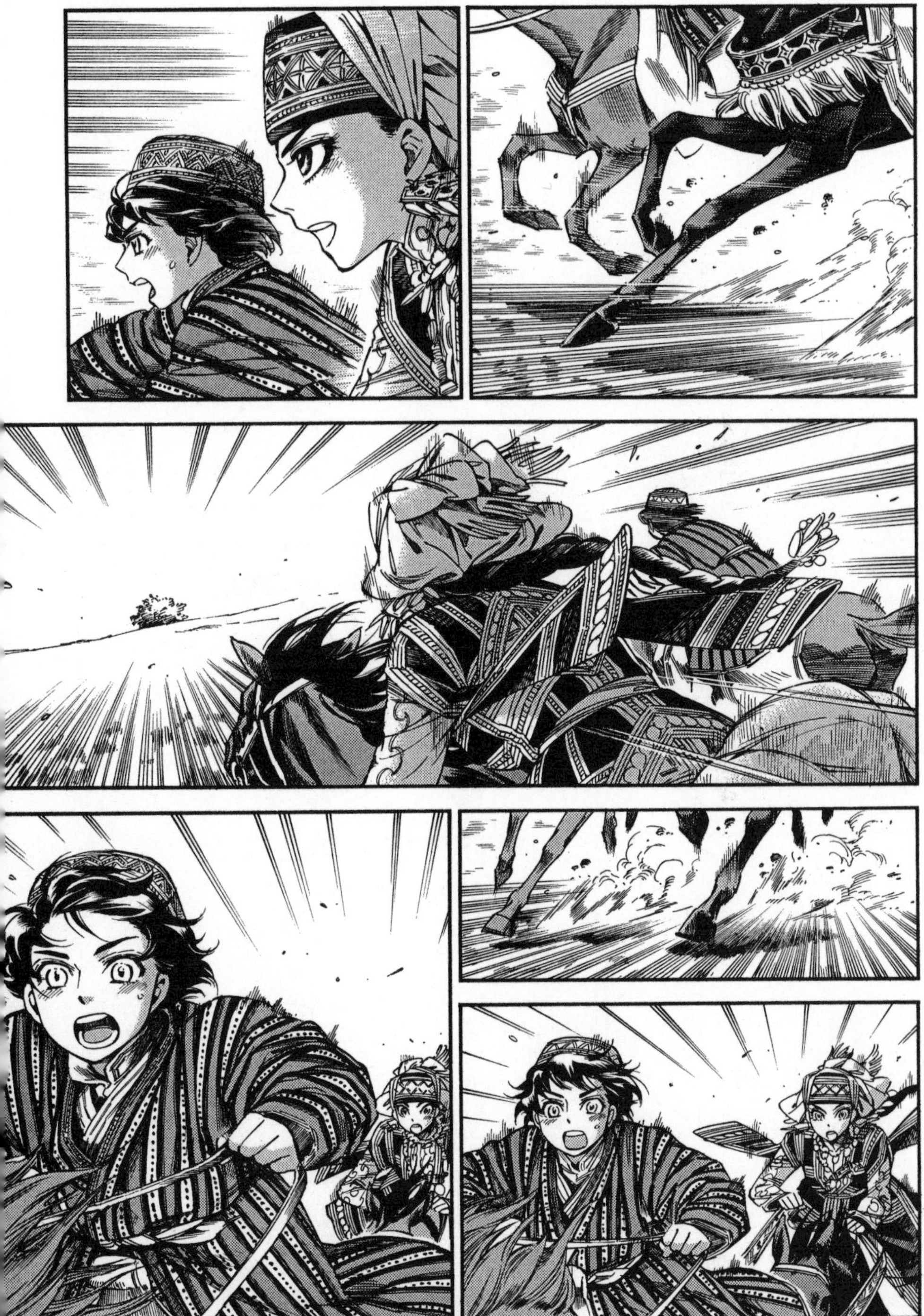

I WON! I WON!
......
YES, I SUPPOSE YOU DID.

HAFF!
HAFF!
THAT'S A LOT OF BAGGAGE.
WHAT DID YOU BRING THAT YOU HAVE SO MUCH STUFF?
...A LITTLE OF THIS, A LITTLE OF THAT.
"THIS AND THAT"?
FAIR IS FAIR.
GO AHEAD AND MAKE YOUR REQUEST.
UM......
HOLD ON A SECOND ...
CAN IT WAIT?
I NEED TO THINK IT OVER.

THIS LOOKS LIKE A GOOD PLACE.
LET'S REST HERE A BIT.

OKAY.
ISO ISO (SCURRY)
MATS.
CUSH-IONS.
TEA.
POT FOR BOILING WATER.
TRAY.
TEA-POT.
TEA-CUPS.
ETC.
ETC.
PLEASE HAVE A SEAT!

SHE BROUGHT ALL THAT?
SO THAT'S WHY THERE WERE SO MANY BAGS...
WELL, IT HAS BEEN AN AWFULLY LONG TIME!
HUH?
ALL WE HAVE TO EAT IS BREAD?
NOTHING ELSE?
I CAN GO FETCH SOME MEAT...
...IF YOU WOULDN'T MIND GETTING SOME WATER BOILING!
OH! OF COURSE.
BE CAREFUL OUT THERE.

DOSA
DOSA (THMP)
WHOA! WHAT A CATCH!
BUT ISN'T THIS TOO MUCH FOR JUST US TWO?
ONCE WE'VE HAD OUR FILL, WE'LL CLEAN THE REST AND BRING IT HOME.
SINCE WE HAVE MORE PEOPLE IN THE HOUSE NOW, THIS WILL SERVE AS TOMORROW'S LUNCH.
OH! YOU ALREADY DRAINED THE BLOOD!

KACHA (KCHAK)
KACHA
GYU (TUG)
I'M FINISHED HERE.
ANY-THING I CAN DO TO HELP?
ALL THAT'S LEFT IS THE DEER...
...I...
I CAN HELP WITH THAT!
IT'S PRETTY MUCH THE SAME AS SLAUGH-TERING A SHEEP, RIGHT?
JUST TAKE CARE NOT TO PUNCTURE THE BLADDER.
EH? WHERE'S THE BLADDER ON A DEER?

IT'S A LITTLE HEAVY, HUH?
DO YOU MIND IF WE TAKE OUR TIME HEADING HOME?
IT'S A HEDGE-HOG!
ODD PLACE TO SEE ONE, HUH?
YOU'RE RIGHT.
AND AT NIGHT TOO.
AMIR, HAVE YOU EVER BEEN PRICKED BY A HEDGEHOG?
NO, I HAVEN'T.
HOW ABOUT YOU, KARLUK?
NOT ME.
I WONDER IF IT HURTS.
TIME TO TRY IT!
NO! AMIR, DON'T!

WE'RE HOME!
WEL-COME HOM—
WELL, LOOK AT THIS!
WEL-COME BACK.
HOW DID IT GO?
WE GAVE THEM A GOOD RUN.
SULKEEK SHOULD BE SATISFIED FOR NOW.
WE CAN'T DO THAT FOR ALL OF THE HORSES, HUH?
I WONDER IF THERE'S SOMEPLACE WE COULD USE AS A RUNNING RANGE.
IS THAT FOR UMAR...
...PARIYA?
UM... YES.
I HAVE TO BRING HIM SOMETHING EVERY DAY WHILE HE'S HELPING OUT...
MOTHER SAID SO...

WE SAW A HEDGEHOG.
A HEDGE-HOG?
I KNOW ABOUT THEM!
THEY'RE ROUND AND GOT SPINES, RIGHT?
THAT'S THE ONE.
AMIR TRIED TO GET ONE TO STICK HER.
I DOUBT IT WOULD HAVE HURT THAT MUCH.
JUST A PRICK AND A LITTLE BLOOD, RIGHT?
EVEN SO, THAT'S NO REASON TO TRY TO GET STUCK.

SAY, AMIR?
WHEN I WON TODAY, YOU SAID YOU'D DO WHATEVER ONE THING I ASKED, RIGHT?
......
...YES.
SO WHAT IS IT?
UM... YOU KNOW...
...I'VE SORT OF BEEN THINKING...

COULD YOU TEACH ME TO SHOOT A BOW?
ALL OF YOUR FAMILY...YOUR BROTHER TOO...ARE REALLY GOOD WITH A BOW, RIGHT?
I WAS THINKING IT WOULD BE NICE FOR ME TO KNOW TOO.
AND IF I DID...
IF YOU DID?
......
WHEN I GOT GOOD AT IT...
...MAYBE I COULD GO OUT AND HUNT WITH YOU......
IT'S A DEAL!
I'LL TEACH YOU!

LET'S MAKE YOU A BOW!
A REALLY STRONG ONE!
IF YOU PRACTICE EVERY DAY...
...YOU'LL BE A SKILLED ARCHER IN NO TIME!
......
OKAY.
KAN KAN KAN KAN (KRRCH)
WHAT'S THAT NOISE?
KAN KAN KAN KAN
KAN KAN KAN
......
WHEN I GET MARRIED ...
...WILL I BE OUT WHITTLING DEER HORNS IN THE DEAD OF NIGHT TOO?

Chapter 49: End

✦ Chapter 50 ✦

CONGRAT-ULATIONS, PARIYA!
ISN'T THIS WONDER-FUL?
BEST WISHES!
YOU'RE SO PRETTY!
YOU MAKE SUCH A BEAUTIFUL BRIDE!

UUUNH! FINALLY PARIYA IS......
AT LAST!
SNIFF!
SNIFF!
AT LAST WE CAN RELAX!
LOOK! YOUR GROOM IS WAITING FOR YOU OVER THERE!
GO TO HIM!

......
MM......
PARIYA ......
YOU......
YOU'VE BEEN A GOOD, QUIET GIRL ALL THE TIME I'VE KNOWN YOU...
...AND I TRUSTED YOU WERE THAT WAY ALL THE TIME.
I HAD NO IDEA THE REAL YOU WAS SO PUSHY.
I GUESS I MISTOOK WHO YOU ARE.

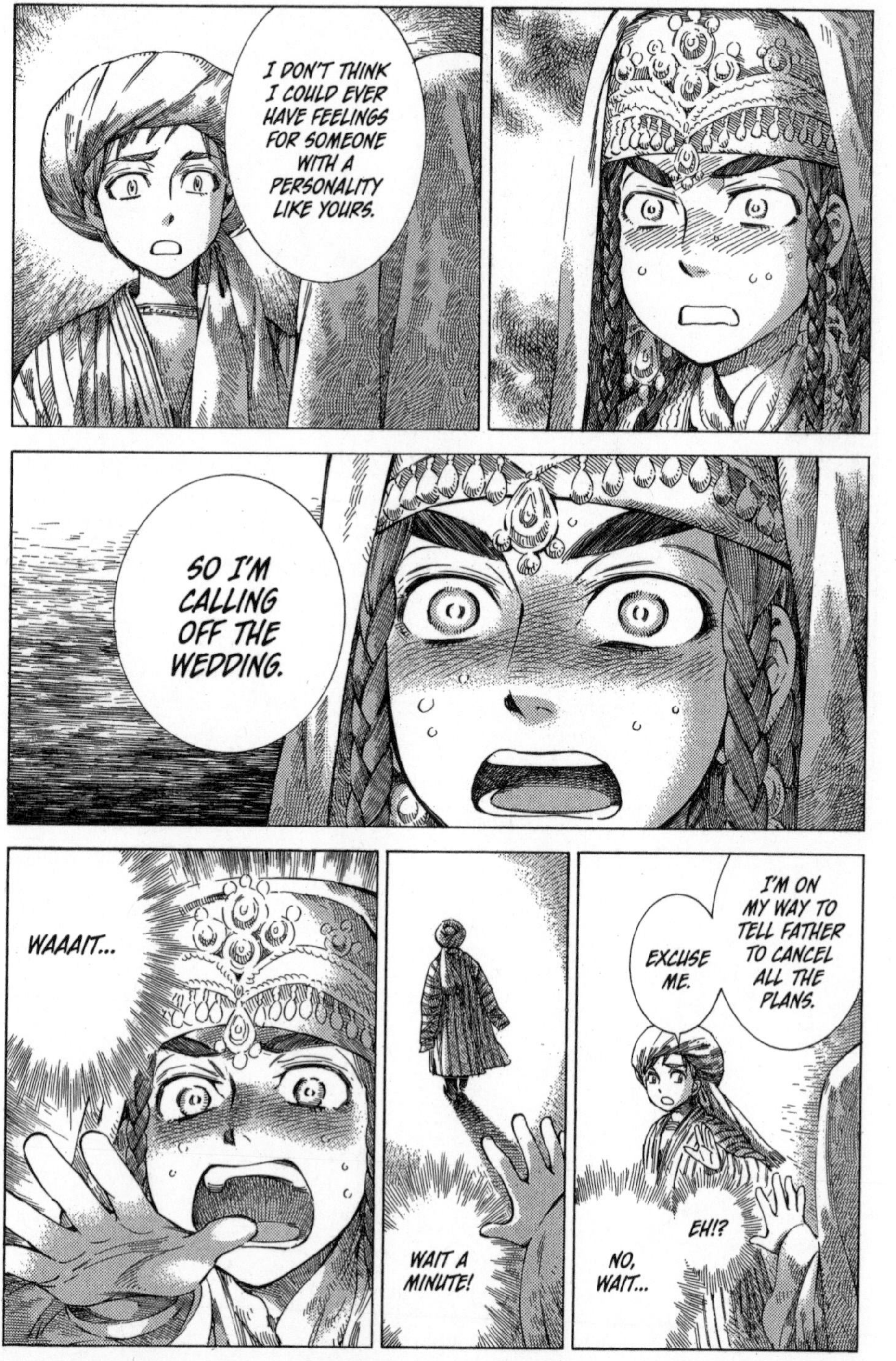

I DON'T THINK I COULD EVER HAVE FEELINGS FOR SOMEONE WITH A PERSONALITY LIKE YOURS.
SO I'M CALLING OFF THE WEDDING.
EXCUSE ME.
I'M ON MY WAY TO TELL FATHER TO CANCEL ALL THE PLANS.
EH!?
NO, WAIT...
WAIT A MINUTE!
WAAAIT...

WAIT!!
HAH!
HAH!
HAH!
HAH!
HAH!
HAH!

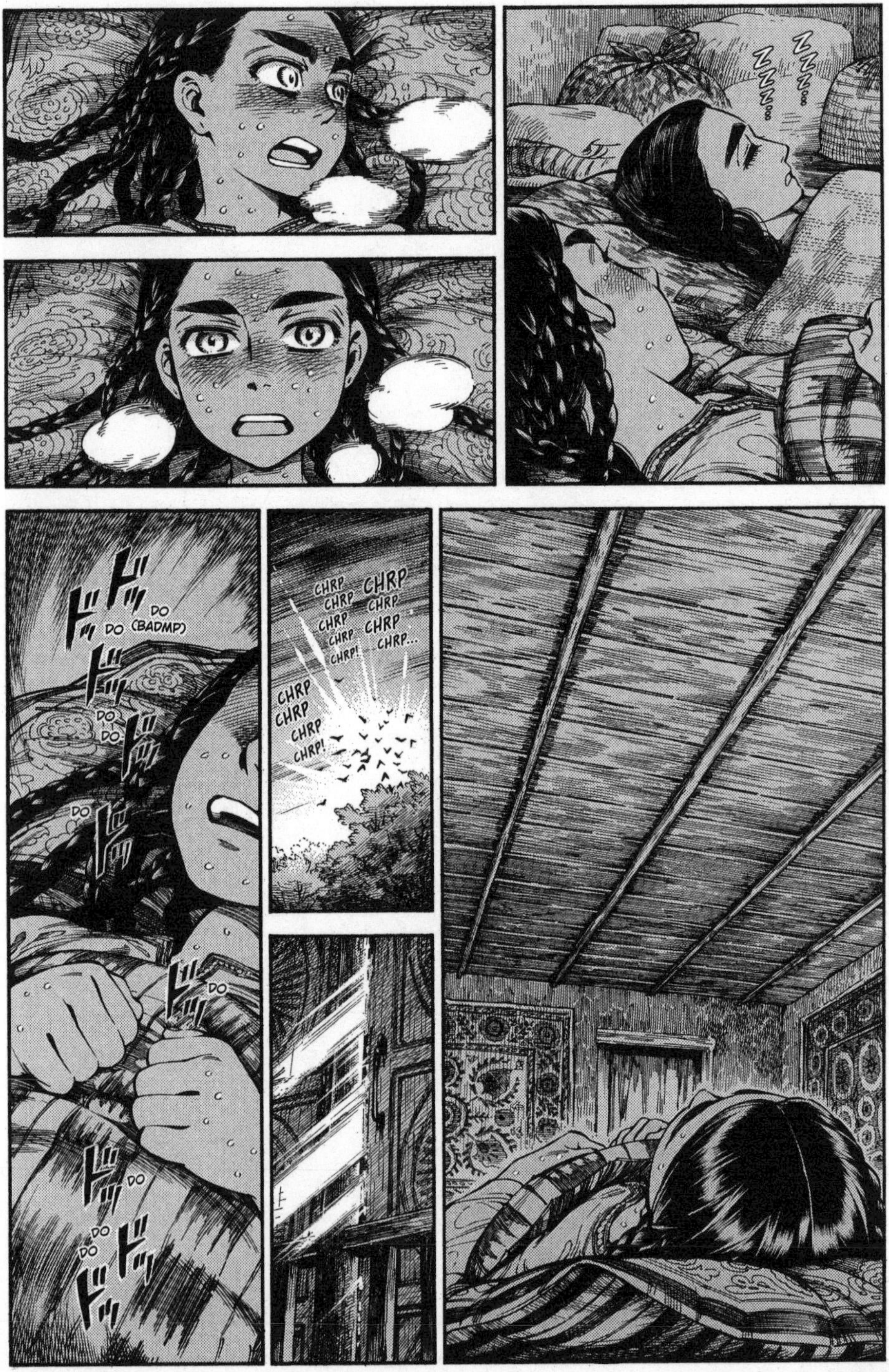

ZZZ...
ZZZ...
ドドドド
DO DO (BADMP)
ドドドド
DO DO
DO
CHRP CHRP CHRP CHRP CHRP!
CHRP CHRP CHRP CHRP...
CHRP CHRP CHRP CHRP!
ドド
DO
ドドドドドド
DO DO DO

......
A DREAM...
WHAT AN AWFUL DREAM...

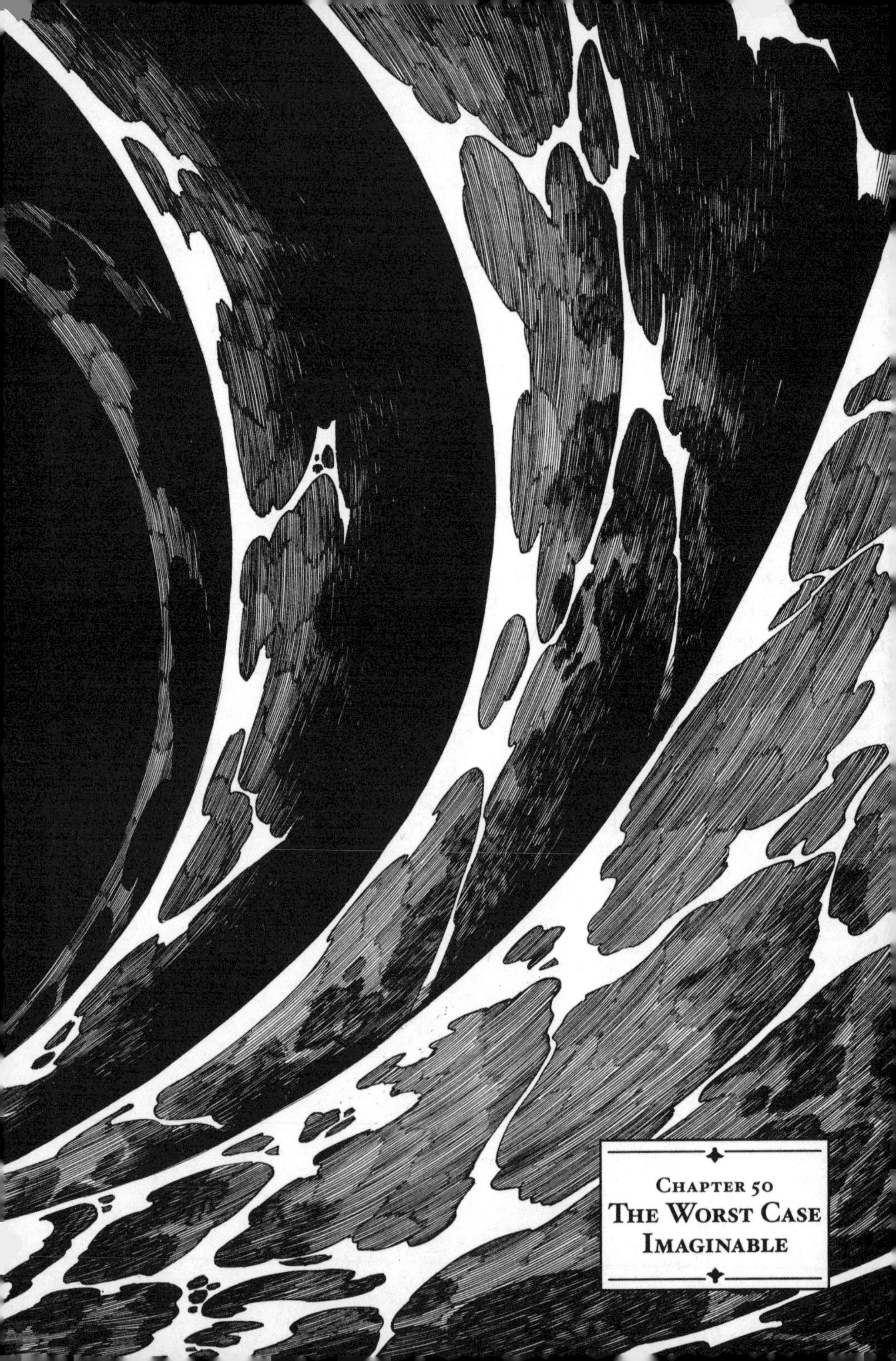

Chapter 50
The Worst Case Imaginable

....
GOOD MORNING.
WHAT'S WRONG, PARIYA?
YOU DON'T LOOK WELL AT ALL.
ARE YOU ALL RIGHT?
......I'M FINE.
IT'S...
...NOT IMPORTANT...
I'LL FORGET IT SOON, SO DON'T WORRY.
REALLY.
BASHA
BASHA (SPLASH)
GOOD MORNING!
MORNING!

WILL YOU BE WITH UMAR AGAIN TODAY?
YEAH. I PROBABLY WILL.
I DON'T THINK I COULD EVER HAVE FEELINGS...
...FOR SOMEONE WITH A PERSONALITY LIKE YOURS.
NO! THAT WAS A DREAM!
JUST A DREAM ......!!
CLUCK! BUK!
CLUCK!
BY THE WAY, WE HAD A DISCUSSION AT THE TOWN MEETING...
I WAS HOPING YOU MIGHT HELP US WITH THE IRRIGATION DITCHES.
IRRI-GATION DITCHES ?

WE'VE BEEN MEANING TO DO IT FOR A WHILE, BUT...
...IT HAD TO BE PUT OFF DUE TO ALL THIS OTHER WORK.
IF WE DON'T DO SOMETHING SOON, THEY'LL GET BLOCKED.
BUT THE MEN HAVE NO TIME.
WE WERE HOPING THAT THE LADIES' CIRCLE MIGHT BE WILLING TO LEND A HAND.
PER-HAPS...
IT SHOULDN'T BE TOO MUCH FOR US.
ESPECIALLY IF WE CAN GET THE CHILDREN TO HELP.
IT SEEMS TODAY THE WOMEN WILL BE DOING OUTSIDE WORK.
SIGH.
......I SUPPOSE SO.
MOST OF THE MEN WILL HAVE PASSED ON THE MESSAGE TO THEIR WIVES BY NOW...
...SO ALL THAT'S LEFT IS TO DISCUSS IT AMONG YOUR-SELVES IN THE LADIES' CIRCLES.
VERY WELL.

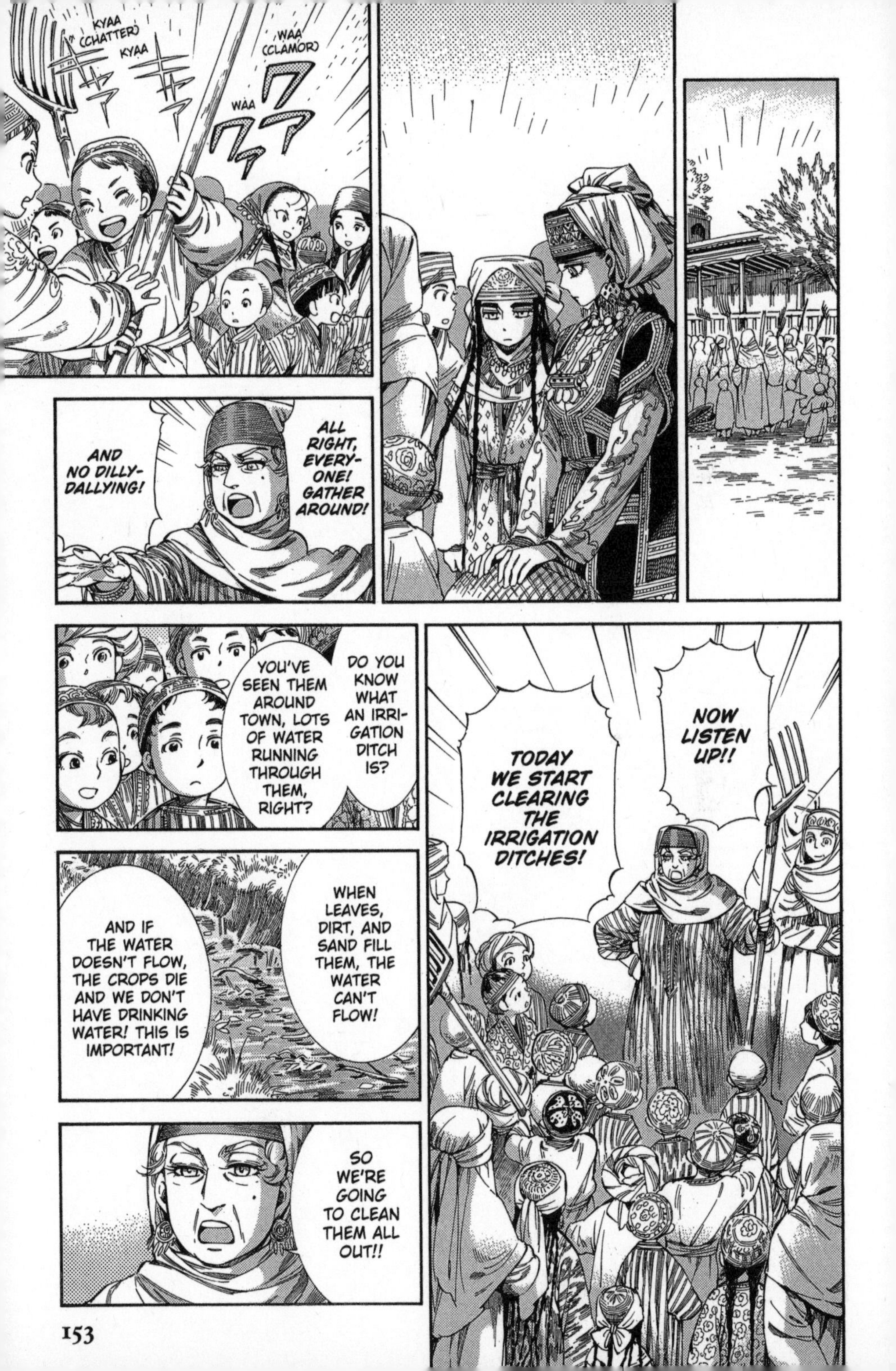
KYAA (CHATTER) KYAA
WAA (CLAMOR) WAA
ALL RIGHT, EVERYONE! GATHER AROUND!
AND NO DILLY-DALLYING!
NOW LISTEN UP!!
TODAY WE START CLEARING THE IRRIGATION DITCHES!
DO YOU KNOW WHAT AN IRRIGATION DITCH IS?
YOU'VE SEEN THEM AROUND TOWN, LOTS OF WATER RUNNING THROUGH THEM, RIGHT?
WHEN LEAVES, DIRT, AND SAND FILL THEM, THE WATER CAN'T FLOW!
AND IF THE WATER DOESN'T FLOW, THE CROPS DIE AND WE DON'T HAVE DRINKING WATER! THIS IS IMPORTANT!
SO WE'RE GOING TO CLEAN THEM ALL OUT!!

YOU ARE NOT TO GO OFF AND PLAY ON YOUR OWN! YOU WILL DO THE JOBS YOU ARE ASSIGNED!
DO YOU HEAR ME!?
YES, MA'AM!
YOU OVER THERE, TAKE THE HALF OF THEM ON YOUR SIDE.
THE REST OF YOU, OVER HERE......
ARE YOU SURE YOU'RE ALL RIGHT, PARIYA?
YOU LOOK LIKE YOU COULD USE SOME REST......
NO, I'M OKAY. I'LL DO IT.
......I WON'T BE MEETING ANY MEN TODAY ANYWAY.
I'M FINE. TRUST ME.

KYAA (CLAMOR)
KYAA
IT'S CERTAINLY A LOT CLEANER THAN BEFORE.
MAYBE WE'RE ALMOST DONE.
WHERE'S PARIYA?

ALL FINISHED OVER HERE!!
OH? THAT WAS FAST!
AREN'T YOU FINISHED THERE YET!?
HERE, I'LL HELP!
ZASSHA
HYAAAAA!
ZASSHA (ZLOOSH)
PARIYA IS FULL OF ENERGY.
WHAT GOOD'S LEAVING A JOB HALF-DONE?
LET'S HURRY AND FINISH THIS UP!

WATCH!
THIS IS HOW YOU DO IT!
GOTO (CLATTER)
ゴト
GOTO
ゴト
GOTO
ゴト
GOTO
ゴト
GOTO
ゴト
COULD YOU WAIT HERE A MOMENT?
SURE.

ARE YOU DONE OVER THERE!?
ALL DONE!
HOW CAN YOU CALL THAT DONE!?
THERE'S PLENTY LEFT IN THERE!
WE'RE DONE!
PARIYA, IT'S ALL RIGHT.
ALL WE NEED IS FOR THE WATER TO FLOW.
AS LONG AS WE GOT MOST OF THE DEBRIS OUT, WE'RE FINE.
EH?
BUT......

IF WE GET TOO PICKY, WE'LL NEVER BE DONE.
BUT...
PARI-YA!
DO AS YOU'RE TOLD.
IT'S FINE TO BE ENTHUSI-ASTIC...
...BUT YOU HAVE NO RIGHT TO ACT LIKE YOU'RE IN CHARGE.
ボン
BON
ボン
BON (BOING)

AH......
AH......
DO (DOOM)
WHY ...!?
HOW LONG...
...HAS HE BEEN THERE ...!?
I HAD NO IDEA...
...YOU WERE SO PUSHY.
NO......
UM...
THIS ISN'T...
SORRY TO KEEP YOU WAITING.
LET'S GO.

WAIT!
AH...
W—
WAIT!
PLEASE WAIT...

PARIYA?
PARIYA, WHAT'S THE MATTER?
✦ CHAPTER 51 ✦
ARE YOU ALL RIGHT?
....

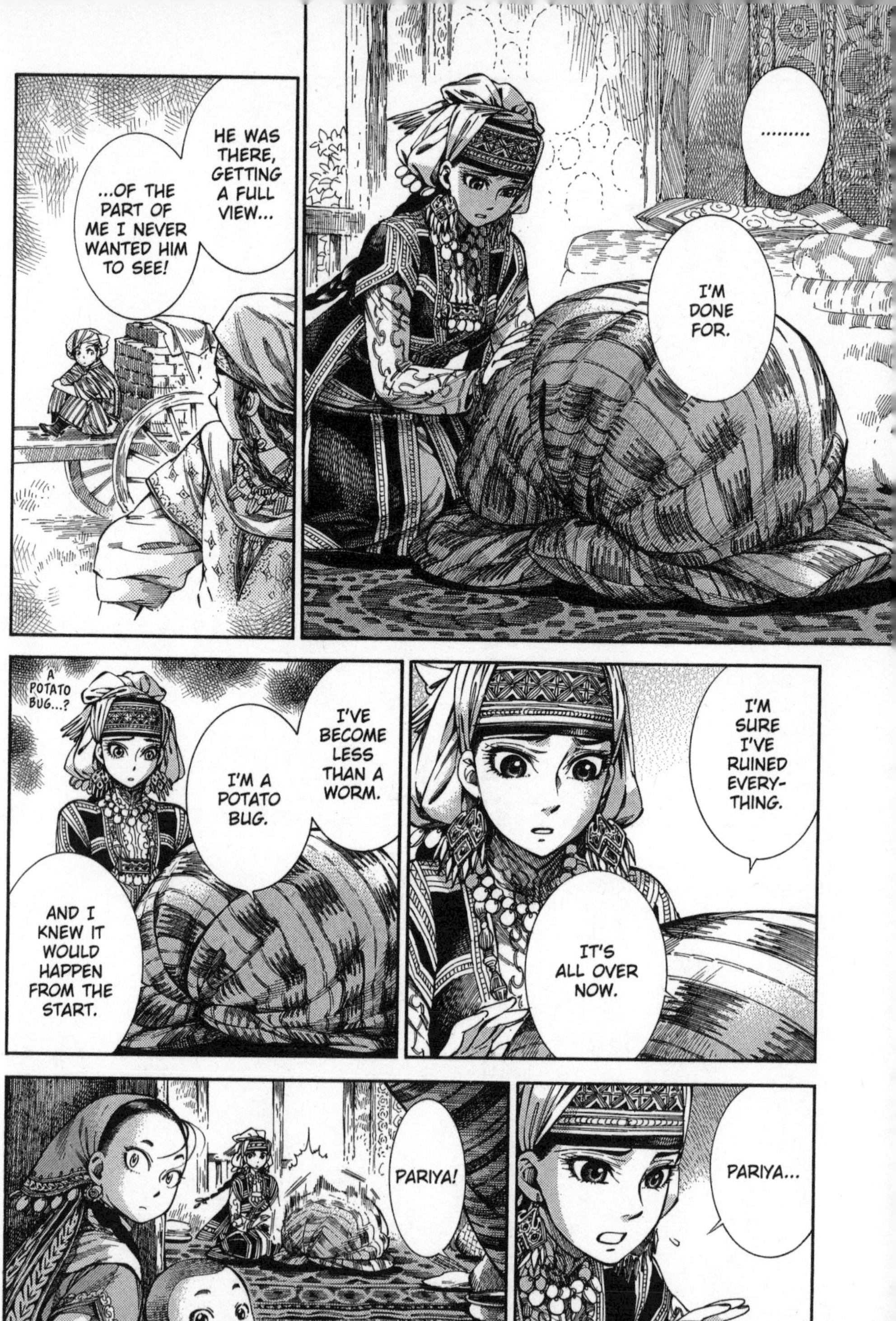
....
I'M DONE FOR.
HE WAS THERE, GETTING A FULL VIEW...
...OF THE PART OF ME I NEVER WANTED HIM TO SEE!
I'M SURE I'VE RUINED EVERY-THING.
IT'S ALL OVER NOW.
I'VE BECOME LESS THAN A WORM.
I'M A POTATO BUG.
AND I KNEW IT WOULD HAPPEN FROM THE START.
A POTATO BUG...?
PARIYA...
PARIYA!

I WENT AND DELIVERED THE USUAL BREAD AND FRUIT TO UMAR TODAY.
WHAT'S THE MATTER? WHY WON'T YOU SEE HIM?
HE SEEMED WORRIED ABOUT YOU.
......
WHY? DID HE SAY...
...SOMETHING ABOUT ME...?
NO, NOTHING IN PARTICULAR.
HE SAID, "SEE YOU TOMORROW"...
COME TO THINK OF IT, HE DID ASK IF YOU WERE "ALWAYS LIKE THAT."
DID SOMETHING HAPPEN TODAY?

ALSO, UMAR WANTED US TO HAVE THESE.
HE SAID HE'S RECEIVED SO MUCH FROM US, HE HOPES WE ENJOY THESE IN RETURN.
THEY LOOK DELI-CIOUS.
ISN'T THIS A GOOD SIGN?

......
WHAT DOES IT MEAN...?
AFTER SEEING ME AT MY WORST...
...MAYBE IT ISN'T ALL OVER?
IS SHE ALWAYS LIKE THAT?
NO.
NO, NO, NO, NO!
I CAN'T RELAX YET......
HE'S STARTED TO DOUBT ME!
IT'S ONLY A MATTER OF TIME UNTIL THE WORST HAPPENS ......!!

I CAN'T JUST LET IT HAPPEN......
I'VE GOT TO DO SOMETHING ......!!
I...
...HAVE TO CHANGE WHO I AM!
I HAVE TO BECOME THE IDEAL ME!

THE IDEAL...
THE IDEAL...?
MOYA (POOF)
MOYA
MOYA
PON (POP)
NO. THAT'S SETTING MY SIGHTS TOO HIGH EVEN FOR AN IDEAL.
THAT ISN'T TRUE AT ALL!
BUT MAYBE... SOMEONE WHO CAN DO...
WHO CAN DO JUST A LITTLE BETTER THAN ME...?

Chapter 51
Pariya's Decision

KAMOLA OF THE RAHIM FAMILY...
A BRIGHT PERSONALITY, ENERGETIC, KIND TO EVERYONE, AND REALLY GOOD WITH KIDS.
AND ALL THE OTHER GIRLS HER AGE SEEM TO RESPECT HER.
AND IT'S NOT JUST HER ABILITY TO SEW AND KEEP HOUSE...
SHE HAS A REAL TALENT FOR SINGING AND DANCING.
OF COURSE HER FAMILY IS PRACTICALLY FIGHTING OFF THE SUITORS.
VISITORS COME TO HER FATHER PRETTY MUCH EVERY DAY.

KAMOLA REALLY IS THE FINEST YOUNG LADY IN TOWN!
I'M SO JEALOUS OF HER MOTHER!
OH, SO AM I!
A GIRL LIKE THAT IS A RARE GEM!
WITH A CHILD LIKE KAMOLA, A MOTHER WOULD HAVE NO WORRIES AT ALL!
NGH!
AS FAR AS I KNOW...
...THERE ARE NO GIRLS IN THE NEIGHBOR-HOOD WITH AS GOOD A REPUTATION AS HERS!
IN OTHER WORDS, IF I CAN MANAGE TO BE LIKE HER...
KA (FLASH)
...THEN I'LL BE ONE STEP CLOSER TO THE IDEAL ME!!

UM... MISS PARIYA?
WHAT'S WRONG? IS THERE SOMETHING YOU WANTED?
N-NO, NO!
NOTHING REALLY...
OH, JUST PRETEND I'M NOT HERE!
I'M JUST WATCHING TO SEE IF I CAN PICK UP ANY HELPFUL TIPS!
I WAS JUST WATCHING!
SO JUST LEAVE ME ALONE!
IT ISN'T LIKE I WANTED TO TALK TO YOU OR ANYTHING!

MOTHER ...
...I THINK MISS PARIYA DOESN'T LIKE ME. WHAT DID I DO TO OFFEND HER?
OH, PARIYA?
THAT'S HARDLY A SURPRISE.
I MEAN, THOSE TWO...
...ARE COMPLETE OPPOSITES.
OF COURSE PARIYA WOULD COME TO HOLD A GRUDGE.
SHE'S BEEN COMPARED TO KAMOLA QUITE A BIT.
AND THINK OF ALL THE MATCHES PROPOSED TO KAMOLA!
THAT CAN'T SIT WELL WITH PARIYA, CAN IT?
......
PARIYA, DEAR...
THE GOSSIP ALL OVER TOWN IS THAT YOU HATE KAMOLA AND ARE GIVING HER THE COLD SHOULDER.
IS IT TRUE?
EH!?
WHY WOULD PEOPLE THINK THAT!?
NO! NO!
COMPLETELY WRONG!
REALLY?

FIRST...
...I'LL WATCH HOW KAMOLA DOES THINGS AND MEMORIZE IT.
I CAN'T DO THIS!
OH, THIS!
YOU MUSTN'T PULL SO HARD ON THE THREAD.
YOU STOP HALFWAY THROUGH.
I CAN'T!
OF COURSE YOU CAN! DON'T WORRY!
TRY ONE MORE TIME.
I CAN'T! YOU DO IT!
YOU CAN IF YOU DON'T RUSH.
LET'S DO IT TOGETHER.
POINT ① KAMOLA IS EXTREMELY PATIENT.

THANK YOU SO MUCH FOR TEACHING HER!
OH, BY THE WAY, I'VE FINISHED THE SEWING YOU ASKED FOR.
OH MY! ISN'T THIS WONDER-FUL!
YOU REALLY DO HAVE TALENT!
GOODNESS, I'M AFRAID THERE'S LITTLE MORE YOU CAN LEARN FROM ME.
NO! I COULDN'T DO IT WITHOUT YOU!
AND MY SEWING IS STILL SO...
POINT ② KAMOLA IS HUMBLE.

COME HERE.
KAMOLA IS KIND TO ANIMALS.

KAMOLA KNOWS HOW TO BE POLITE TO ELDERS.
WHAT GETS LONGER THE MORE YOU CARVE AWAY ITS BOTTOM...
...AND GETS BIGGER AS YOU TAKE AWAY ITS SIDES?
GUESS THE RIDDLE!
UM...
A WELL?
SHE IS EXCEPTIONALLY SMART.
YOU GUESSED IT!
I CAN'T GO ANY CHEAPER.
OH PLEASE, WON'T YOU TAKE OFF A LITTLE MORE?
IT WAS LESS EXPENSIVE JUST A LITTLE WHILE AGO!
AND IF THE PRICE WAS JUST SLIGHTLY LOWER, I'D BUY THE WHOLE THING!
AND SHE'S GOOD AT HAGGLING.
JUST THE TINIEST BIT MORE!
ALL RIGHT.

I SEE IT ALL NOW!
I THINK I UNDERSTAND!
SO... TO BE MORE LIKE KAMOLA, I HAVE TO...
...GET BETTER AT ENDURING STUPID PEOPLE, BE HUMBLE, BE KIND TO EVERY-ONE...
...RESPECT MY ELDERS, GET SMARTER, AND BECOME GOOD AT HAGGLING!!
......
......
......

PARIYA?
KAMOLA IS HERE.
SHE SAYS SHE CAME TO TALK TO YOU.
EH?
...HELLO?
EH!?
WHAT !?
AWAWA (PANIC)
アワワ
WHY!?

UM...
I THINK I MUST HAVE DONE SOMETHING REALLY BAD TO OFFEND YOU, MISS PARIYA... DID I?
IF I DID, I WANTED TO COME AND APOLOGIZE...
N...
NO, YOU DIDN'T!
YOU DON'T HAVE ANY-THING TO APOLOGIZE FOR!
WHAT WAS GOING ON THESE PAST FEW DAYS...
...WAS BECAUSE OF SOME-THING THAT HAS NOTHING TO DO WITH YOU!
IT WAS ALL JUST A MISTAKE!
...REALLY?
I'M... I'M SORRY...
...FOR MAKING AN ASSUMP-TION...
PARIYA SAYS THAT SHE WAS JUST TRYING TO LEARN FROM YOU.

THERE WAS...
...SOME-THING THAT WAS KIND OF WEIGHING ON MY MIND.
I WAS JUST WONDERING HOW YOU DID THINGS.
I MEAN, YOU HAVE A GREAT REPUTATION, AND EVERYBODY TALKS ABOUT HOW NICE YOU ARE.
THAT ISN'T TRUE! NOBODY THINKS—
NO, IT IS TRUE!
MY PARENTS ARE ALWAYS TELLING ME HOW WONDERFUL YOU ARE.
YOU'RE ALWAYS ABLE TO DO EVERY-THING RIGHT!
AND THERE'S NOBODY WHO DISLIKES YOU!
AND THE TRUTH IS, I'M JEALOUS!

I SEE ... IS THAT IT?
YOU DON'T KNOW HOW MUCH I WANT TO SAY, BUT I JUST CAN'T MAKE MYSELF SPEAK.
I LOOK AT THE WAY YOU JUST COME OUT AND SAY THINGS, AND I'M ALWAYS IN AWE.
BUT... I AM TOO.
......
......

WHY DON'T YOU TWO BECOME FRIENDS?
ONCE YOU'RE FRIENDS, YOU WILL NATURALLY INFLUENCE EACH OTHER.
YOU CAN LEARN FROM EACH OTHER AT THE SAME TIME.
...WOULD YOU BE MY FRIEND?
EH?
...UM... OKAY, I SUPPOSE...
I KNEW IT. YOU DON'T WANT TO.
NO, YOU'VE GOT IT WRONG! I WANT TO! I WANT TO!

UM... UH...
OKAY, THEN...
FRIENDS.
AND THAT'S HOW PARIYA ADDED ONE MORE TO THOSE SHE COUNTED AS FRIENDS.

✦ Chapter 51: End ✦

Afterword

AFTERWORD TAN-TA-DAHH! MANGA!!
Come! Springtime!
(FROM THE HEART!)
AND MAKE IT QUICK!
HELLO, EVERYONE! I'M KAORU MORI!
HAIKU
A WINTER MORNING;
AWAKE, BUT CAN'T LEAVE THE WARMTH;
BED-POTATO BUG.
AND WE'RE ALREADY AT A *BRIDE'S STORY*, VOL. 8!
PARIYA'S CHAPTER HAS BEGUN!
EVEN SO, IT'S ALMOST LIKE THINGS ARE MOVING BACKWARD.
STILL, YOU KNEW THINGS COULDN'T GO SMOOTHLY FOR PARIYA!
WHAT!?
AND THIS TIME, SHE'S MADE A FRIEND NAMED KAMOLA.
SHE MAY SEEM OLDER, BUT SHE'S ACTUALLY TWO OR THREE YEARS YOUNGER THAN PARIYA.
LIKE A VERY SMART UNDER-CLASSMAN.
SHE ISN'T CONSIDERED TO BE OF A MARRIAGE-ABLE AGE QUITE YET.
THE REASON PARIYA TALKS MORE FORMALLY THAN KAMOLA IS BECAUSE PARIYA IS STANDOFFISH TO EVERYONE.
MOST PEOPLE DON'T USE SUCH POLITE LANGUAGE WHEN THEY ARE CLOSE IN AGE.
BONK!
ALSO, IN THE "GAZELLE" STORY, WE SEE THE CASPIAN TIGER THAT LIVED IN THAT REGION LONG AGO.
THEY'VE GONE EXTINCT NOW.
THEY SAY IT WAS A BEAUTIFUL ANIMAL SIMILAR TO THE SIBERIAN TIGER.

NOTE: THE AFTERWORD TITLE REFERS TO "HARU YO KOI," A CHILDREN'S SONG FROM THE EARLY 1900s COMPOSED BY POPULAR SONGWRITERS RYUUTAROU HIROTA AND GYOFUU SOUMA. THE SONG IS ABOUT A CHILD WHO WANTS TO GO OUTSIDE FOR A WALK IN THEIR NEW RED-STRAPPED GETA SANDALS AMONG THE BUDDING PEACH BLOSSOMS.

ANYWAY, THIS MAY BE A LITTLE SUDDEN...
...BUT I FINALLY REALIZED...
...MY DEAREST WISH!!
AND ACTUALLY GOT TO VISIT CENTRAL ASIA!!
YEAAAAAH!
NO WAY!
SINCE WE WERE ON A TIGHT TIMETABLE, I HAD TO LIMIT IT TO THREE COUNTRIES THIS TIME.
I WANT TO GIVE A BIG SHOUT-OUT TO PROCO AIR (THE TRAVEL AGENCY) FOR MANAGING TO PACK SO MUCH INTO MY LIMITED TIME.
KAZAKHSTAN
UZBEKISTAN
KYRGYZSTAN
FIRST WAS UZBEKISTAN.
UZBEKISTAN IS THE MODEL FOR KARLUK'S TOWN.
IT'S NEAR BUKHARA.
AN UZBEKISTAN TREE!!
WHOOOOA!
AN UZBEKISTAN WALL!!
WOOOOOW!
AN UZBEKISTAN DITCH OR SOMETHING!!
HOOOOO!
AN UZBEKISTAN CEILING!!
OHHH!
PARASOL
YOU LOVE YOUR CEILINGS, DON'T YOU, MS. MORI?
JEENA, THE GUIDE
YEAH, I WENT TO SEE THE MOSQUES AND STUFF TOO.
LOTS OF 'EM.
JEENA KNEW ALL ABOUT THEM.
TRY TO ACT INTERESTED, OKAY?
BUT IT'S THE LITTLE THINGS THAT YOU DON'T REALIZE YOU'RE UNAWARE OF UNTIL YOU ACTUALLY SEE THEM.
THIS!!
TEARS OF JOY
THIS IS WHAT I WANTED TO SEE!
AND THEN TO KAZAKHSTAN.
KAZAKHSTAN
ALMATY
TASHKENT
KYRG.
UZBEKISTAN
BABOOM!
KAZAKHSTAN IS BLESSED WITH ABUNDANT NATURAL GAS, SO IT'S A VERY WEALTHY AND DEVELOPED COUNTRY.
S...
SO THIS IS WHAT GAS MONEY CAN DO...!!
I WAS COMPLETELY FLABBERGASTED BY THE DIFFERENCE BETWEEN THE TWO COUNTRIES.

ASIDE FROM THAT, KAZAKHSTAN IS...
BIG!
SINCE KAZAKHSTAN USED TO BE HORSE LANDS, IT WAS THE MODEL COUNTRY FOR AZEL AND THE REST OF AMIR'S ORIGINAL CLAN.
COOL!
I CAN ALMOST SEE THE YURTS.
SOME PEOPLE STILL USE YURTS TODAY.
MY FAMILY OWNS LIVESTOCK.
HORSES, SHEEP, AND THE LIKE.
I EVEN HELPED OUT WHEN I WAS A KID.
THE HORSES LOVE THE GRASS HERE.
MY GUIDE, SAMAL, WAS SO COOL, HE LEFT ME TREMBLING.
T-T-T-TELL ME EVERYTHING IN DETAIL!
HE'S A JAPANESE TEACHER BY DAY.
AND THEN, KYRGYZSTAN.
THE MODEL COUNTRY FOR GRANDMA.
KYRGYZSTAN WAS, LIKE KAZAKHSTAN, A HORSE COUNTRY.
BUT IT'S MORE MOUNTAINOUS.
I STAYED OVERNIGHT IN A TINY VILLAGE IN THE MOUNTAINS.
EVEN NOW, THEY USE HORSES INSTEAD OF MOTORCYCLES.
AN ELDERLY FARMER
OOH!
HORSEBACK RIDING
FALCON HUNTING
BAKING BREAD
PUPPIES
YAP!
YAP!
CHICKENS
APPLES
AND AS I LAY IN BED IN A KYRGYZSTAN GUESTHOUSE...
I'M SO GLAD I DRAW MANGA FOR A LIVING!
...IS WHAT I THOUGHT.
OF COURSE I BOUGHT AS MANY REFERENCE BOOKS AND OTHER ITEMS THAT I COULD, AND BUILT UP MY COURAGE TO HAUL THEM ALL HOME. (THE POSTAL SERVICE IS UNRELIABLE.)
APPARENTLY IT'S BETTER TO JUST BUY A CHEAP TRUNK THERE FOR HAULING BACK YOUR STUFF.
AND SO...
I INTEND TO USE THE RESEARCH AND MATERIALS FROM THIS TRIP TO THE FULLEST IN MY WORK!
SEE YOU NEXT TIME!
YOU PACKED IN THE PANELS, HUH?
THE END

A BRIDE'S STORY ⑧

KAORU MORI

TRANSLATION: WILLIAM FLANAGAN

LETTERING: ABIGAIL BLACKMAN

Yen Press
1290 Avenue of the Americas
New York, NY 10104

Visit us at yenpress.com
facebook.com/yenpress
twitter.com/yenpress
yenpress.tumblr.com

First Yen Press Edition: September 2016

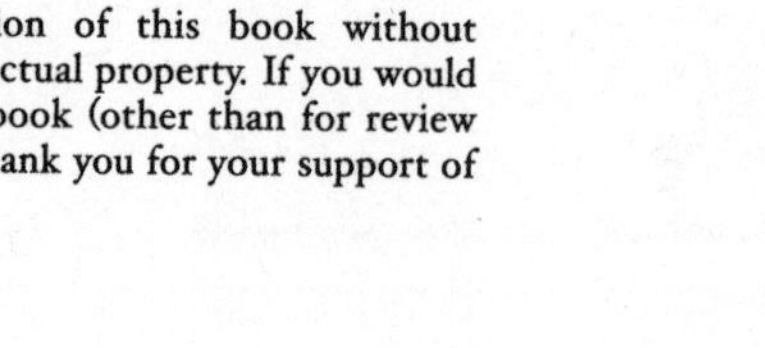

Library of Congress Control Number: 2012450076

ISBN: 978-0-316-31762-7

10 9 8 7 6 5 4 3 2 1

BVG

Printed in the United States of America